Doctor Embalmed

D. W. Fletcher

Poppy Seed Publishers Ltd.

Contents

1

An Invitation

Tony Marshton leaned back in the large armchair. With crossed legs and an air of polite attentiveness, he re-read the letter he was holding in his left hand. Down below in the streets of London, the traffic boomed and bustled. People in all walks of life hurried about their usual business with their usual London air. A real Londoner is easy to pick out, even among a large crowd. There is something about his manner – the purposeful disposition with which he proceeds to his objective, without noticing or caring what is happening around him or who jostles against him.

No one noticed the postman coming out of the large block of luxury flats. He had just left a bundle of letters in the care of the hall porter, who in turn, had hastened to deliver them to their intended doors. Mr Tony Marshton, at number nine on the third floor, had two letters.

The first one was Income Tax. Tony put it behind the clock and two seconds later, had forgotten that he was ever required to pay revenue to the British Government. The second letter was from his Aunt Lucile. Tony has only ever seen his Aunt Lucile once. When he was a young boy, his mother had taken him to stay with Aunt Lucile down at her big country house on the lovely Sussex Weald.

In those days, Uncle Bert had been alive. Much had happened since then. His uncle had died and so had his mother. Three months later, the shock had killed his father too.

Anthony Marshton was made for life, from a mercenary point of view. His mother and father had left him sufficient to spend the rest of his life in luxury and comfort. But, being born with something of the nature of an adventurer, and a smattering of the bravado, he did not find a quiet and peaceful life to his liking. Tony was forever hunting trouble. Not that he particularly liked making a nuisance of himself, on the contrary. But he did like a bit of excitement. So, it was with this intention that he decided to become a freelance newspaper reporter. Up to the present, he had achieved some amazing scoops.

However, the letter in question was offering him a holiday. It sounded like it would be pleasant, beautiful *and* potentially rather interesting too.

Aunt Lucile, in her rather rambling and inconsistent way, was asking him to stay with her for just as long as he wished.

If you find it dull dear, said his aunt's letter, *I won't be offended if you only stay a few days.* Also, it invited him to bring a friend with him.

Tony flung the letter aside, and walked to the window and stood gazing out onto the crowded scene below. Suddenly, he observed a familiar figure proceeding down the pavement towards the building he was in.

Margaret was of medium height, slim and very petite in her manner. She had lovely long, dark curls flowing down from a beautifully shaped head and onto her shoulders. Her face, with an expression of extreme innocence, probably caused by her delicately moulded nose, was extraordinarily striking. She had large, blue eyes and a smooth complexion that had captivated the hearts of many of her friends of the stronger sex.

Tony noted with satisfaction her neat, trim figure and long legs. She was coming to see him! Tony's heart leapt. He had only known her a short while, but he had been struck from the first by her genuine and yet vivacious personality.

He watched her enter the main door below. Tony hurried to answer the knock. He let her in with a cheerful smile on his good-natured face. It was that same good-naturedness that had made Margaret first notice this curly-headed, fair young man.

A mutual friend had given a party and decided to pair these two off. Funnily enough, they had paired off even without their scheming friend's assistance. Margaret had liked Anthony right from when their friend had said, "Miss Palmer – Mr Marshton."

She had taken his hand and looked up into his frank, open face and laughing eyes. He was taller than her by about six inches and she liked his broad shoulders and fit physique. His attractive smile, showing his strong, white teeth sent a tiny thrill shivering up her spine. In three weeks they were inseparable.

As he regarded her now, he longed to take her in his arms and kiss her, but he knew if he wanted to retain her friendship he must wait until he knew her better.

"Margaret," Tony said, "I have just had a letter from my old Aunt Lucile, she wants me to go down and stay with her in Sussex. She has a lovely old manor house, quite near the South Downs. She has also asked me to bring a friend!"

Tony had visions of happy hours spent wandering on the beautiful, green Downs overlooking the sea; of long country rambles with Margaret, holding his arm and smiling up at him. He never thought of the horror and terror he was headed for, or of the ghastly hours of dreadful fear and death that fate had destined him to undergo.

Margaret was charmed with the idea of a long holiday in Sussex, which was her favourite county. If she had only had some forewarning of the terrible experiences that were to haunt her for the rest of her life, she might not have been so keen.

Anthony poured out an egg flip for her and a glass of sherry for himself. Then he gave her his aunt's letter to read, while he went to change the house lounging gown he was wearing for his jacket and waistcoat.

"Let's go down there tomorrow," called Tony impulsively from the bedroom. "I'll send a telegram and we can go first thing in the morning."

"But I promised Teddy Jacobs that I would have lunch with him tomorrow," called back Margaret.

"Then that settles it," declared Tony, coming back into the room, "we will leave on the ten eighteen from Victoria!"

Margaret's pretty face broke into a roguish grin. "What about Teddy?" she asked flippantly.

"Damn Teddy!" retorted Tony.

"Are you sure your aunt won't be put out, having a woman?" asked Margaret. "I mean, she probably meant another fellow, who could share a room with you. She might not have sufficient accommodation for me."

Anthony laughed, "The place is so big, that you will most likely get lost in it!"

"Well, if you're sure that it will be alright, I would love to come," Margaret replied excitedly. "I had better fly home and get something packed, let Mother and Dad know, and tell Teddy Jacobs that I shan't be able to see him tomorrow."

"Good," said Tony shortly. "That fellow always did get on my wick. Can't understand how you put up with him."

Margaret giggled, "I believe that you are jealous."

For an answer, Tony gave her a gentle, playful dig in the ribs.

Margaret rose to go. "Where shall I meet you?" she asked.

"Outside Victoria Station at ten o'clock," replied Tony.

"Till then!" Margaret offered a slim, gloved hand.

Tony smiled at her, holding her hand just a minute longer than was really necessary.

He let her out and stood at the door of his flat, watching her walk down the corridor. At the corner, she turned and waved her hand to him. He waved back and entered his flat.

Directly after he had shut the door, he crossed quickly to the window and flung it open. He thrust out his head and waited for her to reappear at the base of the block of flats. After a minute, she came out and walked quickly down the street, winding her way in and out of the crowds. Tony watched her every movement. Mind telepathy is a remarkable, active element, and it is only a fool who doubts its existence.

Suddenly, Margaret stopped and turned, looking up at the window of the flat. Tony saw her turn and even as her eyes caught his, he swiftly withdrew, and with a bright flush, like a naughty school boy caught stealing jam, he slammed the window down.

Margaret smiled to herself and seeing a passing taxi, she raised her hand. When it drew up by the curb, she got in and was rapidly lost to sight among the traffic.

2

An Ominous Introduction

Mrs Lucile Agnes Sophia Guyate regarded the large cream tea rose quizzically.

"Oh! Ah!" she muttered to herself. "Very lovely, but they do drop so badly, perhaps it will look better where it is."

She walked slowly in the direction of the house carrying the enormous bunch of June roses in her left hand, and her garden knife in her right hand.

As she left the rose garden and came round the clump of laurels by the lily pond, she saw her butler hastening down the path from the house with what looked like a letter in his hand. Upon catching sight of her, he doubled his pace and came up to her, red faced and panting.

"If you please, Madam, this telegram just arrived for you," he gasped, "the boy is waiting to know if there is an answer."

The butler, Mr Skeels by name, was tall and extremely thin. He had an almost completely bald head and little mutton-chop whiskers down the side of his cheeks, hereby showing that if his hair wouldn't grow in the usual place, it would in the unusual. He was invariably dressed in a dark suit with a boiled shirt front and a smart bow-tie. He very seldom changed his placid expression from the polite and submissive attentiveness that he had permanently assumed.

Mrs Lucile Guyate unhurriedly opened the telegram and read the contents. Mr Skeels edged slowly to the right, and with the slightest possible movement of his head endeavoured, unsuccessfully, to see what the writing said.

"No answer," said his mistress, folding up the telegram and placing it in the pocket of her garden apron.

Mrs Lucile Guyate always wore a green apron for gardening. She was a short woman with silver-grey hair hauled round into a large bun at the back of her head. She had a pleasant face with a ready smile. Her clothes were always rather too long for her, but as her legs stuck out from beneath her dress like two matchsticks, nobody missed much.

Mrs Guyate proceeded up to the house in the wake of the butler. Mr Skeels had worked for the family for a great many years now, and he was almost an old family retainer. He had been Herbert Guyate's personal servant and when the doctor had died, Skeels had volunteered to take the post of butler.

Herbert Guyate had been a medical practitioner during his lifetime. He had been a noted Harley Street specialist before retiring and settling down at *Wuthering Winds*, this lovely old Sussex manor house beneath the South Downs. He had died eleven years ago, and from that date onwards, Lucile Guyate has developed a great desire to learn and dabble in the deep and rather murky facts concerning spiritualism. That Mrs Guyate had a bent for spiritualism was known for many miles around.

In the tiny village of Haywards Hill, which was situated some three miles from *Wuthering Winds* by road and about one and three quarters by foot over fields, many rumours were told of strange and mysterious happenings up at the manor.

The inhabitants of this particular piece of rustic England were still very feudal in their ideas. To them, the people dwelling in *The Manor,* as it was always called locally, were to be respected and revered at all times. Whoever they might be.

Dr Guyate had been well known in the district, although he had only lived there about four years before he died. The typical country Sussex folk had liked his cordial manner and admired his slightly superior carriage when in their presence.

As Lucile Guyate walked up the steps, leading through the French windows into the library of *Wuthering Winds*, she distinctly heard the voice of her stocky and none too feminine cook, Mrs Barkley. "What was in that telegram, Mr Skeels?"

"That is none of your business either, Barkley," replied the butler.

"Well, don't try and tell me you didn't 'ave a darn good go trying to find out," retorted the cook.

Skeels made some inaudible reply and the voices petered out as the servants returned to their own duties. Mrs Guyate smiled gently to herself as she arranged the flowers in a large blue vase on the piano.

Suddenly, a figure silently entered the library and stealthily approached Lucile as she bent over her flowers humming softly to herself. The figure was that of a tall, lean, stern-looking woman of about fifty years old.

She might have been younger as her long, plain, black dress and greying hair gave her a look of age. However, her skin was still as young as it was smooth. Lucile Guyate was unaware of the presence of another person in the room until the newcomer, standing behind her, put out a cold, hard hand and touched her on the shoulders. As she did, the sun went behind a cloud and from the bright cheerfulness of the June sunshine, the world suddenly seemed to become dark and dull.

Lucile Guyate shuddered, and with a jolt, she dropped the flowers she was holding. She spun round and with a face which was pale and distorted with pain, faced the dark woman. Immediately, as she recognised the woman, she seemed to crumple up. She sat down heavily on a nearby chair, clutching her hands across her bosom.

"My heart!" she gasped. And then, seeing the other woman uncertain of what to do, she said, "I'll be alright in a minute. Do you mind getting me a drink of water?"

The woman left the room, and summoning Skeels, demanded a glass of water. "Your mistress has had another turn," she said in her rich, deep voice.

Skeels appeared to be very upset and dashed to the kitchen, returning in a few seconds with a glass of cold water.

The woman in black took it without a word and swept into the library again. When she arrived, Lucile seemed to have almost recovered, and the sun had commenced to shine again with renewed brilliance.

"Thank you," she smiled, "so silly of me." In her good-naturedness Mrs Guyate had completely forgotten the unnecessary cause of her relapse. If she had not forgotten, she gave no sign that might have given her guest any room for embarrassment.

Roma Beaumont regarded her hostess, and in a sense also her employer, with half-closed black eyes and an unsmiling face. "I am so sorry," she said mechanically. "It was my fault really."

Lucile smiled in denial. "Of course not," she replied. "But never mind, I have some news to tell you. Let's go out on the veranda."

They went out onto the terrace and sat down in two deck chairs. "My nephew and his friend are coming to stay with us here for a while," said Mrs Guyate.

Roma Beaumont did not answer but kept her eyes averted from her friend's face. She sat there looking out across the lawn to the swimming pool which was sur-rounded by lovely weeping willows.

Lucile regarded her friend with a puckered brow. "You do not seem particularly pleased," she said pleas-antly.

For the first time Roma looked her companion direct-ly in the eyes. "You know that Dr Guyate might resent the presence of strangers," she said coldly.

"But my nephew is not a stranger," argued Lucile. "He knew my dear husband when he was a boy, and his presence might encourage Bert to materialise again. I will get him to try and help us," she finished, looking rather pleased with her suggestion.

Swiftly, like a lithe, black cat, Roma Beaumont leaned forward and grasped her friend's arm in a grip of excep-tional strength. "No!" she snapped, her tone firm and authoritative. "Tell them nothing, nothing at all, either of them. They might cause me to fail entirely."

"Well, if you say so," submitted Lucile.

Roma appeared relieved. "Good," she said as she once more leaned back in her chair. "That is most impor-tant."

The two women sat in silence for some minutes gaz-ing absently over the beautifully laid out garden.

"How do you think you are getting on? When do you think any real reaction will come to your efforts?" Lucile asked slowly and with obvious emotion.

"Have you had any more dreams?" replied her companion, giving Lucile a swift glance and then once more averting her eyes from the placid, kindly face. The question was clearly to evade the original subject.

Mrs Guyate took the bait. "Yes," she said in the same quiet way, "only just last night I dreamt that Bert came back."

Once more, the woman in black leaned forward. "What happened?" she enquired, changing the tone of her voice to a soft, persuasive and rather attractive note. She took the other's hand and sat holding it, looking earnestly into her eyes.

Mrs Guyate spoke in a low voice, almost a whisper, "He came back, do you hear – he came back."

"What did he do?" asked Roma.

"He came out of his cabinet. He came across the hall and started up the stairs. When he got to the top he came along the passage and – and –"

"Go on!" snapped the other.

"He tapped on my door. Tapped on the panels for me to come and speak to him," finished Lucile.

"What happened then?" inquired Roma Beaumont, flashing her dark eyes over her shoulder. An eavesdropper would spoil the whole scene, at this critical moment of their conversation.

"Then I seem to forget anything else that happened."

"Did Dr Guyate return to the cabinet?"

"Yes," answered Mrs Guyate. "I seem to remember that he was there as usual in the morning."

"Is there anything else that might have any bearing on the subject?" asked the other woman. "It is most important that you tell me everything, no matter how insignificant and how obscure it seems to you."

"Well," said Lucile slowly, "there is one thing, but I don't suppose that it has anything to do with it," she ended shortly.

"Tell me!" demanded Roma, in her deep voice. "I must know all, if through my medium I am to materialise Doctor again."

"'Tis only a little thing," said Lucile, "but if you say I had better tell you, I will."

The dark woman nodded assent.

"Vaguely, I seem to miss something of Herbert's," she continued. "What it is, I don't know, but some possession of his or some article he was fond of, has gone."

She laughed shyly and dropped her trance-like manner, returning immediately to her usual good-natured heartiness.

A soft breeze ruffled the graceful shrubs on each side of the veranda. "Was there nothing more?" asked Roma.

"Nothing," answered Lucile.

The sound of the luncheon gong resounded through the manor. The two women rose and went into the house.

3

Guests at the Manor

The sleepy, wayside station of Little Barlow lay basking in the strong, June afternoon sunlight. The green fields of clover and young wheat were delightfully varied by patches of cool, shady copses. A streamlet trickled its glistening water over the tiny pebbles that lay in the track of gently moving water.

The station master of Little Barlow was old Joe Wiggens. He was sitting on the empty box propped against the wall of the miniature ticket office. His hat pulled well down over his eyes and his chin sunk down onto his chest. Joe Wiggens liked the warm sunshine, and although he would not have admitted it for worlds, he was sound asleep.

Suddenly, the dreamy silence of the peaceful scene was shattered by a voice – a rough, deep, musical voice with a typically Sussex accent. "Hey Joe! Wake up!"

Joe Wiggens sat up with a start, and with a somewhat dazed look, gazed round him, trying to fathom where the hail had come from. Then he saw the man leaning on the fence surrounding the small station.

"Hello there, Jim!" The old stationmaster smiled a friendly greeting to the labourer. He rose to walk over to the fence for a chat.

The farm worker who was dressed in rough working clothes with heavy boots and leggings, said in his loud voice, "N'ays, yer forgotten the eleven five, Joe?"

Joe Wiggens commenced with fumbling in the large pockets of his waistcoat for his family's only heirloom – a massive gold watch. It had come to Joe when he was forty-three. Joe had never quite got over the thrill of pulling it out of his pocket and gazing at it proudly in front of the villagers assembled in the *Clucking Hen* on a Saturday evening.

Joe Wiggens started to go through this procedure, opening the cover with a grunt of satisfaction. Jim Hardy gazed with admiration written all over his honest, weather-beaten face.

"Due in about ten minutes," he announced with an air of importance, replacing his watch in his pocket. The two men stood leaning against the white painted fence.

Jim still with beads of sweat sparkling on his brow from the exertions of hedge cutting and ditch digging. Joe held his little green flag. Both looked up the line, for the appearance of the London to Brighton (stopping all stations) train.

The first sign was white smoke appearing over the top of a belt of trees that obscured their view of the track. With a roar, the train pulled up in the station. Faces appeared at the windows. Joe and his companion watched two young people climb out and slam the door behind them.

Joe spoke to the engine driver, and the train started moving off again. "Them two must be going to *The Manor*," said Jim.

"'Ow do you know?" asked Joe suspiciously.

"Well," Jim scratched his head, "Mrs Guyate had a telegram yesterday, you know." Joe nodded. News travelled fast in those parts and a telegram was a rare event.

"That there telegram was read by the butler, Mr Skeels, you know 'im?" continued Jim. Joe nodded again. "Mrs Guyate left it in the pocket of 'er gardening apron," revealed Jim, "and after reading it, Mr Skeels told Mrs Barkley what it said. Well, Mrs Barkley told the house maid and the housemaid, Jenny Walker, who goes out with that young fellow who works for Farmer Jackson, told 'im and 'e told me in the '*En* last night." Jim paused for breath.

By this time the young couple had reached the men. Joe shambled forward to collect their tickets.

"Can you tell me where *Wuthering Winds* is?" the young man asked.

"O! *The Manor*," returned Joe, giving Jim a knowing look.

"It's down the road, yonder," he said, pointing out of the station. "Or you can get there over that there footpath," he went on, indicating a rough track.

"How far?" asked the young man.

"Three miles by road, and one and a bit by the track," specified Joe, inspecting their tickets.

"Thank you," the young man replied, grimacing at the young woman. "And is there any means of transport around here?"

"Not unless you get Farmer Hawkins to drive you there in 'is trap," answered the old station master. "And the village is a mile from 'ere."

"Very well," said the young man. "Thank you for your trouble."

"Not at all, Sir," said Joe Wiggens pleasantly.

"We will have to walk," said the young man to his companion when they reached the road. "Shall we go by the road, or by the footpath, Margaret?"

"By the footpath, Tony," answered the girl, shaking her dark curls to the back of her neck, with a toss of her head. They set off along the dusty track, Tony carrying their large suitcases, one in each hand. Margaret carried her handbag and another little hat box under her right arm, and a smaller case in her left hand.

Joe Wiggens and Jim Hardy watched the laden couple turn the bend in the winding footpath. It was not until then that they noticed that another passenger had alighted from the train. He was a short, plump man in his early forties. He was wearing a rather loud check suit and a herring-bone patterned swagger coat. He had a green pork pie hat perched precariously on top of his brown hair that was receding from his temples, exposing a broad forehead. He had with him a large travelling case and a small briefcase. He stood on the platform, mopping his brow and waving to Joe at the other end of the platform.

"Porter, come here," he called. Joe did not move.

"Ticket collector, I want you!" shouted the little man, waving his short arms about more than ever.

Joe gave no sign nor gesture that he had heard.

"Hey! You!" bellowed the small man, with the trace of an American accent. "Come and give me a hand, will you?"

This time Joe ambled towards him, muttering to himself about the crowds of trippers nowadays.

"Where's *Wuthering Winds*?" demanded the man.

Joe Wiggens grudgingly indicated the footpath. "A young man and a lady just gone up there," he told him. "They are going to *The Manor*, if you hurry, you'll catch 'em up."

The well-built man, staggering slightly under the weight of the suitcase, hastened up the footpath after the couple.

Margaret gazed at the lovely countryside spread around her. Her deep blue eyes sparkled and flashed with joy with the contagious feeling of springtime. The skirt of her smart travelling outfit swung around her knees as they walked side by side in silence up the country lane. A nesting blackbird flew from a nearby bush with an echoing shriek, betraying the fact that its young were hidden in that particular hedgerow.

They reached the stile and Tony put all their baggage over first. Then, with a swing of his long legs, he vaulted the stile and put out his hand to assist Margaret over. Margaret took the offered hand and stood on the lower bar of the stile. As she stood there regaining her balance, her eyes caught Tony's and she realised he was regarding her with a tender attentiveness. She stood, still holding his hand, looking at him.

"Isn't it lovely?" she exclaimed impulsively. "It makes you feel glad to be alive! To hear the birds singing and see the green fields and know that everything is bursting forth into flower and fruit with the coming of the spring, Tony. We are going to have a gorgeous time down here. I sort of feel it."

Anthony Marshton looked up at the sweet face so close to his. "My holiday will be perfect if you are with me," he replied.

"You sweet boy," returned Margaret.

Slowly, his face and hers had drawn closer together. With her lips so close to his, Margaret felt her heart beating exceptionally fast. With his hand holding hers, Tony felt spring's sweet message to the young surging through his veins. His head was swimming, her eyes were closed as she waited for the touch of his lips on hers. Suddenly, the sound of a voice made them draw swiftly apart and Margaret jumped quickly over the stile.

"Are you going up to the house called *Wuthering Winds*, folks?" asked the little man with a nose rather too large, in a slight American accent.

Tony, with a guilty flush, looked at the newcomer with an annoyed expression. The cheek of the fellow butting in like that right at that moment!

"Yes," he answered curtly.

The gentleman regarded their luggage. "Looks like you're going to stay too," he observed with a friendly inquisitiveness that annoyed Tony more than ever.

"Well folks, meet Wilbur D Mortimer," he said, extending a hand to Margaret with a polite, if somewhat over-confident, air. Margaret shook hands and he jumped over the stile. Tony said nothing, and with only the usual formalities, they continued all together.

The first view of the house, with its five straggling gables, was most attractive. Standing in extensive grounds, with a modern swimming pool on the lawn, and a delightful maze of paths winding round its beautiful gardens, *Wuthering Winds* captivated the imagination of all three of the people. They saw the side of the slope that led gently down to the big wrought iron gates fronting onto the road.

They did not realise that when they entered those gates they were starting on a chapter of their lives that all three of them would have done anything to escape.

Mr Mortimer led the way down onto the road. They entered the grounds by the little wicket gate in the high wall that surrounded the whole estate. Together they walked up the drive to the house. Mr Skeels answered their knock.

"Mrs Guyate is expecting you," he told them. "I am very pleased to see you, Mr Anthony," he said sincerely.

They crowded the entrance hall and started removing their hats and coats, handing them to Skeels. A door leading into the hall opened and Mrs Lucile Agnus Sophia Guyate appeared.

Mrs Guyate was wearing a long green frock with a house jacket of crochet lace. Her usually neat grey hair was slightly ruffled. She had been reading one of her many books on spiritualism, and the excitement had caused her hair to become untidy, with the constant dabbling it had received. Mrs Guyate always fiddled with her hair when she read books on spiritualism, and as these were the only books she ever read, it was not surprising that her hair sometimes was very untidy.

She was obviously very surprised to see her guests, and for a moment was undecided whether to withdraw and tidy her hair or whether to pretend not to notice that it was messy. Eventually, she made up her mind to apologise.

"Hello!" she exclaimed, her plump face lighting up with a warm smile. "So glad you have come. Sorry I look so dishevelled," she went on. "How are you, Tony? Haven't you grown!" Mrs Lucile Guyate flung her arms around the neck of the startled Mr Wilbur Mortimer.

"Not me, lady, it's him," said the American, indicating Tony who was looking at his Aunt and watching her movement closely .

She is heavier and seems more absent-minded than she used to be, he thought. Instead, he beamed, "Aunty, how are you? I am pleased to see you again. This is Miss Margaret Palmer – a friend of mine." He took Margaret's arm and gently guided her towards his aunt. Margaret shook hands with the old lady, charmed by her friendly manner.

"I expect you all want a good wash and change," she said. "I have a room for you each. Dinner will be at seven," she continued, leading the way across the hall to the base of the high, thickly carpeted staircase.

As they walked after Lucile Guyate, Tony noticed that the massive grandfather clock was showing twenty minutes to six. They followed his aunt up the staircase. Tony also noticed that all the walls were covered with dark oak panelling. There was a great, carved bannister post both at the base and the top of the stairs. On the wall, all the way up the stairs at regular intervals, hung life-sized portraits of priceless paintings in beautiful frames. On the narrow landings, as they went up, Tony saw valuable, giant vases on tiny tables with finely carved legs of black Indian ebony.

At the top of the stairs, Mrs Guyate paused and pointed, "Batchelors wing to the right." Then, turning to Margaret, said, "Will you wait here a second, my dear?" Margaret smiled in agreement, and then gave Tony a communicative look.

As they strode along the panelled corridor, the two men – one short and robust, and the other tall and lithe – noticed a figure standing in a window bay.

His footsteps made no sound as he stepped forward with a discreet bow. The dignified butler asked which rooms the gentlemen would have.

"The first and second," replied Mrs Guyate, without turning her head. Skeels followed them with their luggage.

For the first time, the American spoke. Tony had noticed that he looked rather bewildered since he had entered the house. Now he spoke to Tony in an undertone, evidently so that the old lady would not hear.

"How in Pete's sake did that guy get up here with our things?" he asked.

"Up the backstairs," answered Tony curtly. He wondered just who the small man was and what his business was here.

Mrs Guyate swung open the door of the first room they came to. Tony indicated his bags and Skeels left them in the room. "I'll be in the drawing room room," said his aunt, "and before dinner I would like a little chat with you about your doings since we last saw each other."

The American, followed by the butler, passed on to the next room. Tony opened his bags on the enormous four poster bed and unpacked his clothes into the big tallboy. He quickly washed and changed into evening dress. A few minutes later, he left his room and made his way down the stairs.

Meanwhile, Mrs Guyate had come back to Margaret who was standing and waiting at the head of the stairs. "I have got you a room near mine," she said, as they followed Skeels along the opposite side of the corridor.

The butler deposited Margaret's suitcase in the middle of the room, and after a few kind remarks of smalltalk, the old lady left.

Margaret pushed the heavy, oak panelled door closed and gazed about her. The entire house seemed to have the same dark panels. She could not see any electric light and rightly presumed that *Wuthering Winds* was without this modern blessing.

The room was large with a bay window stretching right across one wall. She noticed there was a wash basin and towel on an old-fashioned washstand. She looked at the massive four poster bed with a feeling of awe; she had never slept in anything like that before. The uneven floorboards were covered by a skin rug. An ancient dressing table stood in one corner; the mirror reflected a sunset from over the elm trees by the tennis court. A heavy carved chair stood next to the low table by the bed. Both these articles were made of the same dark wood as the wall panels.

Somehow the room depressed Margaret's cheerful spirits. It had mysterious corners and latticed windows that obstructed some of the light from completely filling the room. Margaret washed and changed into a long crimson gown.

***

"Oh! There you are, Tony," said his aunt, as he sauntered into the front drawing room.

He seated himself on the settee beside her. "You haven't written since your mother and father died," stated Aunt Lucile.

"I have often meant to," replied Tony apologetically, "but I have never actually done so. I wish I had now."

Their conversation continued on these lines, until Margaret and Mr Wilbur Mortimer entered the room, both looking refreshed and elegant.

Tony thought the girl looked lovely in her gown and noticed the split skirt, which exposed a slender white ankle and calf.

"Anthony," said Mrs Guyate, "you never told me your other friend's name."

Tony looked at his aunt in astonishment. "He is no friend of mine – that is to say," he added quickly, realising his rudeness, "I have never met this gentleman before."

"I thought this was too good to be true, folks," chimed in the American. "I wondered why I was given such a remarkably hospitable reception. I couldn't make out why I was given a room and an invitation to dinner. Actually," he continued, "I am Wilbur D Mortimer, representing the *Morning Star Insurance Company*." He produced a card from his waistcoat pocket and offered it to the world in general. Nobody took it. They were all too astonished!

"I thought…" began Lucile Guyate, and then sat down weakly and shut up. Margaret laughed aloud. After a moment Tony followed suit.

The old lady began to speak again. "There are no more trains stopping here until next Monday," she said. "They never stop on Saturdays and Sundays, and today is only Friday."

The short man grinned from ear to ear, but did not answer. Then the old lady smiled pleasantly. "There's only one thing for it," she said. "Mr – er – Wilbur must stay the weekend with us."

If the American could increase his grin at all, he did so. Fate had played right into his hands; he could not have dreamed of better luck. "I promise to be a good boy," he chuckled, "and thank you very much, Madam. You are Mrs Lucile Guyate, aren't you?"

Tony's aunt nodded. "I am. How did you know?"

"They told me at the office," he replied. "Now, can I interest you in a tidy life insurance policy, or perhaps a fire, burglary, or accident policy? Have you ever considered the wonderful compensation offered by my company, *The Morning Star Insurance Company*? It's..." At that moment Skeels appeared, framed in the doorway.

"Dinner is served, Madam," he announced with dignity and retired discreetly.

"Well," said Mrs Guyate, "we'll see about that later. Let's go in for dinner."

When they reached the huge dining hall, which was dimly lit by candles in large chandeliers and candlesticks, they noticed that there was a figure already seated at the immense, polished oak table.

"This is Miss Roma Beaumont, a friend of mine," said the old lady. The woman rose, and was dressed in another black silk gown. Her long, black hair dangled on her slim shoulders. Sitting all alone in the candle-lit, oak panelled room, she looked rather mysterious and unearthly.

She greeted them all with only a flicker of a smile. Her finely arched, dark eyebrows lifted about a fraction when she learned who the plump, little man was.

Dinner was a quiet affair. Mr Wilbur Mortimer did most of the talking on matters concerning insurance for the largest part of the meal. Margaret and Tony kept exchanging glances. Miss Beaumont said almost nothing. Skeels wafted in and out with the dishes.

When they had finished, they rose together. "We will go to the music room," Mrs Guyate informed her guests.

They proceeded across the hall. Margaret was slightly behind them when they turned the corner of the hall and went into a room on their right. Margaret hurried to catch them up, but not having seen where they had gone, she continued straight down the passage and entered a room at the end.

Suddenly, the silence of the great house was shattered by a ghastly, shrill scream.

Everyone rushed to the end room. They found Margaret standing in front of a large, glass cabinet in which stood the motionless figure of a man.

"What is it?" she gasped in terror.

"It is Doctor Guyate," said the old lady. Observing Tony's stunned look, she added, "When he died eleven years ago, I... had him embalmed!"

4

Doctor Guyate

The guests stood rooted to the ground. With the exception of Mrs Lucile Guyate, they stared in astonishment at the glass cabinet. Roma Beaumont did not appear interested once the echoes of Margaret's horror-stricken scream had died away.

The figure was that of a man of medium height with exceptionally broad shoulders. He stood upright, one hand resting across his well-defined chest. His evening suit was impeccably tailored, complemented by a crisp white shirt front. Yet, it was his face that captivated attention – so striking that it seemed to linger in the mind's eye like an apparition, even after it had been briefly glimpsed.

The dead body of Doctor Guyate stood embalmed, in a coffin-shaped cabinet, with a glass door completely covering the front. The door had a small metal lock which was quite unique in design and shape.

The vacant, chilling eyes of the dead body seemed to pierce through the room, straight across the long, oak panelled library, through the glass doors of the bookcase, past the covers of the dusty old books and through the walls of the manor house. They continued their unblinking gaze across the stretch of lawn, through the high walls surrounding the grounds, across the rugged South Downs, the straggling seashore, and out over the sea, as if the body of the departed spirit was seeking an escape to join the soul and leave the earth behind forever.

Doctor Guyate's forsaken body had a small, grey, pointed beard and a neatly trimmed moustache protruding from his skin. His penetrating, stone-coloured eyes were bridged by bushy eyebrows of the same grey as his beard. His complexion was beautifully preserved with just a hint of too much colouring in his parchment-like skin. The cheeks were still well hued, but the forehead had little lines creeping in. The hands however, had developed a rather nasty brown, wrinkled appearance and the slightly too long fingernails were slightly cracked and split in places.

His shoes still boasted the perfect shine from when he was first enclosed in his terrible casket. A stark, haunting display, for the body stood exposed for all to see. The living eyes could now look upon the dead eyes, the expressionless face that seemed almost to twitch, as if the thin purple lips could still speak.

The corners of the mouth were slightly drooping and the lips were slightly parted in the centre. Strong, yellow teeth could be seen clenched together, firming the muscular development of the powerful jaw. Indeed, a more striking man would be hard to find!

Despite his cold, stern face, there was still a trace of kindness. His well shaped, slightly curved nose suggested great strength of will. His head was scantily covered with iron grey hair and a vein stood out boldly on his broad forehead.

He had a thick, powerful neck with little rolls of skin hanging in tiny lines either side. It was only small points like these that gave the impression of age, and was such a distinguishing feature about the ghoulish and somehow rather dreadful figure.

Small wonder that whereupon, Margaret in her unprepared condition, had cast her beautiful eyes on the cabinet and its terrible contents, that she had opened her mouth and uttered a horrible, blood-curdling scream that was even now, only just losing itself among the old tapestries hanging from the panelled walls of the dingy, but somewhat enchanting room.

Was it enchanting or was it merely magnetic? Powerfully magnetic and appealing in its ghastliness? Was it the room? Or was it the unusual and frightening occupant that it contained within its ancient walls? Fear alone can tell the answer, for fear alone holds the unconquerable attraction that compels the human mind to believe in the unseen!

As the guests recovered their composure, Mrs Lucile Agnes Sophia Guyate, the person who had known the embalmed man better than anyone, spoke.

"Yes, my dears," she shared, "that is Herbert, my beloved husband. He died when he was sixty-six. He was all I had. Our only child was lost to me when she was only a tiny baby. I could not bear to lose Herbert, I always wanted to be able to see his face before me and to be able to touch him if I really wanted to."

Seeing the subtle flinch of the others, she added, "Yes, touch him if I want to. You see that tiny lock there?" she pointed with a finger, shaking with emotion, "I have the only key that there will ever be to fit that lock. If I want to, I can unlock that cabinet and get Herbert out – but I have never done so. To be able to see him always, whenever I want to, is enough. To feel that he is in this house with me, under the same roof, that is sufficient."

The tension of the room was almost unbearable, punctuated only by the ticking of the great marble clock that stood on the mantelpiece above the enormous open hearth, where the bare, red bricks glowed softly in the fading light of the June evening.

The oppressive silence was finally broken by Tony, who had clearly seen enough to subdue his aroused curiosity, for the moment at least.

"Let's go back into the music room, shall we?" he asked quietly. Without a word, the company moved towards the door and returned along the passage, turning into the brightly, candle-lit room on the left.

But it was to be noticed that Margaret kept as close to Tony as possible. Unbeknown to her, the terror of *Wuthering Winds* had only just begun!

5
The Missing Photograph

That night Margaret slept lightly and somewhat uneasily. She tossed and turned in the big, four-posted bed before dropping off into a troubled doze. As she slept, she dreamt. Her imaginative brain kept a recurring thought going round in her mind. Just what she dreamt she could not remember when she awoke in the morning, but only that she had dreamt a dreadful dream, filled with weird shapes and unseen figures, ghastly corpses and dead eyes staring, staring, staring...

She could vaguely remember an experience as a young girl. She dreamt of a shape she had seen somewhere before, it was walking towards her and she could not move. She couldn't think what the shape was nor where she had seen it before, but that it was there she could not doubt. It was coming closer, closer, nearer, nearer...

Margaret Palmer sat up with a start. For a moment she could not think where she was, then looking about her, she remembered she was at *Wuthering Winds* in Sussex. Her agile mind quickly recalled all the things that had happened to her since she had arrived. She wondered what it was that had woken her up. She thought that she could remember some slight noise that had disturbed her troubled sleep. She glanced at the door.

Bright moonlight flooded the chamber. With a swing of her slim legs, she threw back the covers and leapt barefooted out of bed. Throwing a dressing gown about her slender shoulders, she hastened to the massive oak door. Grasping the iron ring that served as a handle, she pulled it open. Clad only in her thin night attire she felt the keen night air.

Suddenly, she heard footfall along the wide passage! She stepped out onto the landing and looked along the corridor. It was with a feeling of mingled astonishment and relief that she saw the black gowned figure of Miss Beaumont.

Her dark hair was let down onto her shoulders. Her face showed surprise at seeing Margaret standing and regarding her with amazement. She stopped. The bright moon shone white and ghostly upon the figures of the two women.

"I thought I heard something," said Margaret, by way of an explanation. "It must have been your footsteps."

"I was just going down to the library," explained Miss Beaumont.

Margaret stiffened as she thought of the ghoulish occupant of that particular room. Nothing but wild horses could have dragged Margaret down to that room at this time of night.

Miss Beaumont noticed her agitation and added, "I was going to get a book, I find it difficult to sleep tonight. I think it must be the moon, it sometimes affects me." She smiled at Margaret in a rather sad sort of way. Margaret returned the smile and with some suitable remark, withdrew back into her room.

She looked at the luminous dial of her wrist watch that she had placed on the low table by her bed. It said twenty to three. Had Miss Beaumont been awake all night then? Margaret tumbled back into her bed, and went off to sleep as soon as her head touched the soft pillow.

***

Anthony Marshton strode breezily into the breakfast room of *Wuthering Winds*. "Hello everybody."

Sitting at the table was his aunt, Mr Mortimer and Margaret. Standing in the background, near the great polished sideboard covered with breakfast dishes, was Skeels. The warm morning sunshine made the silver dish covers sparkle and shine, reflecting tiny sunbeams onto the ceiling and walls. A great patch of sunlight fell across the snowy white tablecloth, causing the cutlery to appear to be shafts of glistening gossamer lying on the table like a delightful cascade of sparkling dew.

Mr Wilbur Mortimer had once more taken up the matter of life insurance and other items that his distinguished firm offered to the benefit of the general public. Mrs Lucile Guyate ate her breakfast without appearing to notice the presence of the American at her right elbow. Margaret looked just a wee bit tired, or was it strained, but that fact Tony quickly put down to the strange house and its peaceful surroundings – it was definitely not like London. Tony seated himself at the long table.

"Eggs and bacon, Mr Anthony?" asked the butler from the side-board.

"Rather, Skeels," answered Tony good humouredly, "I feel just like I did when I was here last! What an appetite I had then." Tony noticed a flickering shadow pass over his aunt's face for just a second, then it was gone.

"Tony," she said, "you were just a slip of a boy, but you were always prying into everything you saw. I remember the time you fell into the water-butt by the greenhouse."

Margaret laughed. "His legs would stick out quite a lot now, wouldn't they?"

Mr Mortimer had been talking all the while to the world in general, but now he stopped.

"Isn't there someone missing?" he asked, looking around the table.

"Miss Beaumont," said Margaret quickly as though she had been thinking about the person in question at that very minute.

"She never comes down till late," said the old lady, "one morning not till eleven o'clock."

It was on the tip of Margaret's tongue to tell them about her meeting with Miss Beaumont on the upper landing in the early hours of the morning, but then she thought better of it. She decided to tell Tony when she had an opportunity to be alone with him. She glanced across the table at him. He was dressed in white flannels and a cricket shirt with a striped blazer over them. His curly hair and the healthy roses in his cheeks made him look rather boyish now. Margaret had been undecided what to put on. She had only bought a few clothes as her limited sized suitcase had not allowed her to pack much. Eventually, she decided to wear a light tennis frock, which Tony noticed, nicely set off her figure.

"What about a couple of sets of tennis after breakfast, Margaret?" asked Tony. "That is of course, if Aunty will let us play on her court?" Mrs Guyate nodded and gave a smile of approval.

"I should love to," said Margaret. "It's just the morning for it too," she added, giving him a bewitching smile. She badly wanted to speak to him alone.

After they had finished breakfast, Margaret and Tony rose to go but stopped as the American spoke.

"Say, Mrs Guyate, does the other lady play tennis? 'Cos if she does, perhaps we can make up a foursome. It would be just grand to take a swipe at the old ball again." He chuckled to himself.

"No," returned Lucile. "I don't think she plays."

"Who is she, Aunty?" Tony asked the question in an innocent voice, perhaps just a shade too innocent.

"Oh, just a friend," replied his aunt.

"She doesn't say much," remarked Mr Wilbur Mortimer.

Margaret, with a little flush, suddenly blurted out, "I met her on the c–"

"Good morning," the deep rich voice made everyone in the room turn around and face the speaker. Miss Roma Beaumont stood framed in the doorway. She was wearing a purple frock with white pockets at either breast. Her hair was rolled up tightly around her head displaying a slim white throat and neck. With her dark eyes reflecting the rays of the early morning sunshine, she looked rather attractive in a sleek *cattish* way. She walked to the table with her slender hips moving in perfect rhythm to her body.

Everyone noticed her perfect poise as she seated herself.

Skeels gazed at her for a moment from under his scanty eye-brows before turning abruptly to serve bacon and eggs from the sideboard.

"We were just wondering if you played tennis?" The American broke the silence and relieved a slightly strained atmosphere that had sprung up since Miss Beaumont entered the room.

"No, I don't," she replied without taking her eyes from the plate that Skeels had set before her.

"Oh," said the American and dropped the subject. "Now about this insurance," he started again.

Margaret and Tony left the breakfast room and went out into the hall. They started walking down the passage that led to the library. "We will go out of the south French windows," Tony directed.

He pushed open the door of the room and walked in. Margaret paused on the threshold. "This room gives me the creeps," she murmured.

"Oh that," replied Tony, nodding his head towards the far corner. Margaret went in and took a quick glance over her shoulder. The cabinet was covered with a large black cloth.

Margaret made an attempt to smile as she followed Tony through the doors onto the veranda. Once outside all her fears left her. She didn't know why, but that room decidedly frightened her.

"Strange idea, that," said Tony as they went down the steps and on the velvety grass. "I should have thought it would have helped her to get over Uncle Bert's passing if she had buried him, like most people do. I remember she was frightfully cut up when he went, they were most devoted," he said quietly.

Margaret did not answer.

"She's a bit eccentric like that," he went on, "but a game old stick really."

"How rude you are!" smiled Margaret. "I think she is very sweet."

The fresh, green turf felt springy under their feet. The dew sparkled in the warm sun, seeming to make the most of its chances to beautify the peaceful scene before it was evaporated by the greedy sunbeams. The early bird, out looking for the first worm, twittered noisily. The sky was cloudless as they strode across the lawn. Long, laddered gossamer trails hung from every tree and bush; the air felt cleaner and sweeter with each breath they took.

The strange and unsettling terror of *Wuthering Winds* seemed a very long way off as they entered the wire gate leading onto the hard tennis court. In the small thatched pavilion they found two rather battered old rackets, but nowhere could they find balls.

"Wait here for a second," said Tony. "I'll run back to the house and ask Skeels, he is bound to know where to find some."

Margaret watched his white clad figure, showing up boldly against the green grass, hurry across the lawn. She sat down on the garden seat and waited for his return.

As she sat there, she noticed that there was no wire netting behind the pavilion, only a dense shrubbery. She gazed at the curtain of greenery for a second, then she began to examine the old rackets. Suddenly, she heard a twig snap behind her. Margaret spun round in the seat. She watched the lush, green shrubbery. *Probably a stray rabbit*, she thought.

Then, with hardly a sound, the bushes parted and the sleek, dark head of Miss Beaumont appeared. For a moment she did not see Margaret and continued pushing herself between the shrubs. When she was nearly through, she suddenly saw Margaret sitting there regarding her with a look of astonishment on her face.

For a second, a look of annoyance passed like a shadow over Miss Beaumont's clear-cut profile. "Oh!" she exclaimed. "Are you here?"

Margaret explained that Tony had just gone up to the house to get some balls.

"I'm just having a ramble round," said Miss Beaumont, "I always do after breakfast."

Just then, Tony returned swinging a net containing about half a dozen balls. "I have some," he called. Then, seeing Roma, he stopped. "Hello Miss Beaumont! Have you come to watch us play tennis?"

"No, I am just having a brief walk," replied Roma, and turning rather abruptly she went through the little wire gate and without so much as a glance back, she walked across the lawn up to the house.

"Odd person," observed Tony, wrinkling his good-natured brow. "It seems as if she almost resents our presence here."

Margaret was on the verge of telling Tony about her strange meeting last night with the woman in question, when Tony started to wind up the slightly dilapidated-looking net.

"Let's forget all about her," he said. "It's really of no consequence."

Miss Beaumont walked across the green turf without noticing the delightful signs of summer that had thrilled Tony and Margaret as they had walked over the same piece of ground a few minutes earlier.

That the two young people were in the way here, the dark woman never doubted, as was the ridiculous American. In some way, they must all be removed as quickly and simply as possible, otherwise all the hard work and careful thought that she had spent would be wasted.

As she drew near the house, she noticed that Mrs Lucile Guyate had placed a deckchair on the veranda and was working industriously on a piece of needlework in the sunshine. She looked up as Roma walked up the steps. She greeted her friend with a pleasant smile that was not returned by the other.

Miss Beaumont erected a hammock chair next to the older woman and sat down. For a few minutes she said nothing, then abruptly she started speaking.

"I have changed my mind about your nephew and his friends," she commenced. "They must all be told what my purpose is here and what my presence is designed to do. Under these new conditions my stay here is prolonged."

"Roma, you are always welcome here, under any circumstances," interrupted Mrs Guyate kindly.

Miss Beaumont waved the remark aside, just as though it had not been uttered at all. "Tonight," she continued, pausing dramatically, "I feel that something must happen to bring the matter to a head."

"Just what do you propose to do?" asked Lucile.

"I intend to summon Doctor Guyate's spirit to take possession of his body again."

Lucile started violently, and the colour drained from her cheeks as she nearly dropped her needlework. "He is locked in the cabinet," she said in a far away voice.

"The cabinet must be unlocked," answered Roma. "His body must be free so that his spirit may make use of it – if we can summon his soul to earth again. The other people in the house, with the exception of the servants, must aid us by using their powers of concentration."

"Do you think anything will really happen?" asked Mrs Guyate. She had always said that she believed in the return of a spirit to the physical world, but as yet she had never had any great experience of proof.

Later on at lunch, the American, who had returned from a ramble in the grounds, once more returned to the attack on Mrs Guyate in his endeavour to sell her some sort of insurance policy.

"Have you ever thought what would happen if you kicked the bucket, Madam?" he asked lightly. "One of my clients popped off only a couple of months after taking out a policy with my company, and his next of kin made their fortunes out of it." He signalled Skeels to serve him with some more wine, before continuing.

"Another gentleman purchased fire insurance, and only a year or so later, he lost everything except his pyjamas, when his house caught alight. He had bought another house and two of everything he had before, within a week of his compensation being paid." He swallowed the glassful of ruby-coloured wine in a gulp, then after smacking his lips, he said, "Now Madam, what can I do for you? One of each?"

Mrs Guyate smiled. "I think I would like to go into it a little more before I definitely decide."

"Right you are, Mrs Guyate. I ain't trying to sell you nothing," replied the American sincerely.

Tony laughed, "Aunty, I believe you're being taken in bit by bit."

The subject changed, and talk went into other channels. Suddenly, a frown passed over Mrs Guyate's pleasant face. She pushed back the wisps of grey hair that fell in spirals onto her forehead. For a moment the general conversation ceased.

"It's funny," said Lucile in an abstract way, "I have missed a photo of my dear husband. I suppose nobody has seen it, have they?"

For a second there was silence round the table.

"Not I," said Mr Wilbur Mortimer.

"Nor I," offered Margaret.

"I haven't either," pondered Tony.

All eyes had moved to the respective speaker in turn. Now everyone looked at Miss Beaumont. The tall, dark woman gazed straight ahead of her. The bright sunlight streamed through the large bay windows. Before this minute the atmosphere had been light and genial, now for some unknown reason, there seemed to have sprung up a slight tension.

For about ten seconds the people seated round the table gazed at Roma Beaumont. A shaft of atmospheric sunlight, creating a vivid spotlight, shone on to the sharply chiselled features of the magnetic woman. Without a word, she looked calmly at each of the occupants of the room as they sat waiting for her to speak. Then she fixed her eyes upon her hostess. "The dream," she said quietly, but with a tremor in her voice. "Remember your dream."

For what felt like a full minute, Lucile gazed at Roma, her face working in emotion. She had turned quite white, her thin hands clutched at the table cloth, dragging the flimsy lace nearer and nearer to her. The strain was becoming intolerable.... Her eyes, wild and haggard, gazed at each of her guests in turn.

Suddenly, a glass of wine at her elbow was dragged too near the edge of the table. With a crash, it shattered on the polished oak floor. The red, glossy liquid spread slowly over the boards. With a stifled sob, Lucile twisted in her chair, clutching her heart as the strain became too much. The tension had finally snapped.

6

An Approaching Storm

"Wonder what's going on in there?" mused Mrs Barkley, plunging her brawny, bare arms into the sink where she was washing up the luncheon plates.

Mr Skeels was equally as curious, but his superior dignity prevented him from discussing the matter with the cook and housekeeper of *Wuthering Winds*. Jenny Walker, feeding cutlery into a knife cleaner, watched wide-eyed from the corner as a young man passed the kitchen window, and in the next minute, appeared framed in the doorway.

It was the first time she had seen Anthony Marshton, and from that minute onwards, she was *his* for the rest of her life. She regarded him now with a feeling of awe as though he was a young god. His fair, wavy hair was slightly ruffled by the disturbing events of the last few minutes while the strong June sunlight silhouetted him against the background of trees around the tennis court. He could easily have been Apollo or Hercules.

"May I have a word with you please, Skeels?" he asked pleasantly.

"Certainly, Mr Anthony," answered the butler, leaving the kitchen and stepping out onto the cement path that followed the circumference of the house.

They walked along in silence for several minutes, Skeels keeping a respectful half pace behind Anthony. The powerful sun beat down mercilessly onto the parched earth below. Anthony raised his head and gazed across the lawn to where a glint of shimmering water showed between the little copse's screen of leafy foliage. He resolved to spend a pleasant hour or two in the shade of the lovely piece of wild garden, with Margaret if possible. The thought of Margaret jerked his mind back to the moment.

How was she taking all this? he wondered. Certainly *Wuthering Winds* must seem a strange place, with the peculiar assortment of characters, the unmodernised house and worst of all, the grisly occupant of the gloomy panelled library. The presence of the interfering American had been vaguely disturbing and he hadn't been able to have the heart-to-heart chat with his aunt that he intended to have.

As the two men wandered along the path, Tony watched Skeels carefully. The butler appeared somewhat nervous and rather agitated. Tony wondered why.

"How long has my aunt been having these heart attacks, Skeels?" asked Tony at last, suddenly stopping and turning to face the butler.

"About seven years now," answered the other. "They were not very bad at first but she refused to go to any specialists."

Tony could not help noticing that Skeels seemed very relieved about the direction the conversation had taken.

"She would always go to the local doctor, a Mr Riley by name," continued the butler, "a very nice man but..." Here the butler faltered, raising his scanty eyebrows up and down several times and shooting a quick glance at Tony before continuing. "Well, he has a slight weakness for alcoholic liquor, not that I wish to run down his professional reputation, on the contrary – but I consider that Mrs Guyate was worthy of better attendance."

Tony nodded thoughtfully. He was rather surprised that his question had drawn so much from the usually quiet butler.

"Thank you Skeels," he said after a pause.

Skeels seemed thankful to get away and Tony watched his long, thin figure hurrying back to the kitchen. Tony wondered why Skeels had appeared so uneasy while he was talking with him. Suddenly, all thoughts of the butler were dismissed from his mind as he saw Margaret cross the lawn towards him. Clearly she had been looking for him and she seemed pleased to find that he was by himself.

She came up to him and slipped her arm through his. They walked for a moment in silence and then instinctively headed towards the woods. After a minute, Margaret broke the silence, "Your aunt has gone upstairs to lie down for a while," she said. Tony nodded without replying.

They reached the copse, and taking a narrow path that seemed to lead to the centre of the wood, they pushed their way through the straggling undergrowth. As the cool shadows closed off the glaring sunlight, the sweet scent of the scattered, wild flowers rose up around them and the twittering of startled birds filled the still air. A deep connection suddenly formed between the two young hearts.

Tony sensed Margaret's vague fear of the strange events that had unfolded in the old house, while Margaret recognised that Tony was quietly unsettled and somewhat worried about what their stay might ultimately bring.

Little did they know that every movement that they had made up to this moment, was being observed. High up on the third floor of the house with the twisted gables and lichen covered roof, a distorted face was pressed to the window pane of a tiny room.

The face was that of Mrs Lucile Guyate. It twitched and worked with pain and emotion, with wide eyes that were red-rimmed and watery. She stood there until the two young figures below had disappeared among the green shady foliage. Then, suddenly springing to life, with an agility surprising for a woman of her years, she left the room and hastened down the three flights of stairs. A feat rather remarkable for a person who had barely recovered from an unexpected heart attack!

Upon reaching the ground floor, she hurried along the spacious hall and turning to the left, entered a room which failed to catch any sunbeams for a greater part of the day. Not seeming to notice the dullness and gloominess of the room, she stood in the centre of the floor gazing at an object by the further wall. This was the room that contained the terror of *Wuthering Winds*.

The still stretch of glistening water was adorned with the dappled reflections of overhanging branches. The rush-lined banks, framed by the shaded green undergrowth, captivated Margaret and Tony, holding them spellbound for a long moment.

They seated themselves, side by side, on a fallen tree trunk. Tony gently wrapped his arm around the slim shoulders of the lovely girl who stirred his heart with her closeness. Margaret leaned against the warmth and comfort of his strong shoulder, resting her chin against it.

For what seemed to them an age, but was really only a few fleeting minutes, they remained in this position, looking out over the pool and the peaceful loveliness of the woodland scene.

Together they watched the heads of two pure and lovely white lilies drift slowly closer, floating on the water with the effortless grace that defines the natural beauty of a flower. Then, with a slight shudder, that seemed to radiate the joy of their closeness, the two lilies touched, drew closer and then held each other, as if savouring the fleeting beauty of a moment that could never be recaptured.

Suddenly, the silence of the peaceful scene was shattered by a loud and intrusive voice. "Ah! There you are, I've been looking for you two everywhere." The overbearing American, dressed in plus-fours, stepped forward through the trees.

Margaret and Tony twisted round and looked in the direction of the voice. Tony rose and regarded Mr Wilbur Mortimer with a touch of disdain.

"Whew!" he exclaimed, "ain't it hot," and so saying, he withdrew a large silk handkerchief from his pocket and proceeded to mop his brow. "Listen folks, how about a swim? Mrs Guyate has offered us the use of the swimming pool on the lawn, whenever we want it."

Tony rather resented the little man's manner, as if he were a part of the family, like he was, or as if he was, an invited guest. Tony held his tongue.

"Yes, it would be lovely to bathe," broke in Margaret. "I certainly do feel dreadfully hot."

"Come on, sister!" yelled the American excitedly, and grabbing her hand he started back to the house with a brisk step.

Tony stood for a moment watching their receding figures. Margaret turned her head and gave him a smile and waved to him to come too. He heard them chatting as they moved through the undergrowth. Feeling frustrated and vaguely annoyed, he followed in their wake. The cheek of that fellow barging up and running off with his girl like that!

Suddenly, he checked the flow of his thoughts. *Was she his girl?* She had never said so! Tony resolved there and then to ask her at the very first opportunity. He realised the ticklishness of the question and further resolved to be extremely tactful about the matter.

How could he guess that before the chance came for him to speak with Margaret again, an event would have occurred that was to haunt him for the rest of his life.

Twenty minutes later, a party of scantily clad figures pranced from the house and proceeded across the lawn to the bathing pool.

Eager eyes watched from behind the Aspidistra, which stood in the window of the dining room, as Tony, Margaret and Mr Mortimer sallied out in their bathing costumes to the awaiting water. Jenny Walker, the pert and rather pretty young housemaid of *Wuthering Winds*, gazed at the broad and muscular shoulders of Anthony Marshton and flicked an imaginary tear from her left eye, as she noticed Margaret's neatly proportioned figure in her smart, yellow and green swimsuit.

Mr Wilbur Mortimer presented the comic touch, in a costume that Skeels had dug up from apparently nowhere. It hung in a long flowing skirt about his pink, podgy knees, and although his body filled the costume to overflowing outwards, there was little doubt that it would have taken two Mr Mortimers to fill it downwards.

They found that Mrs Guyate and Roma Beaumont were seated in the shade of the laurel hedge talking together in low voices. Tony's aunt looked up cheerfully and said, "We've come to watch you swim, who is going to be first in?"

Margaret dipped her toe playfully into the water. "Oh!" she exclaimed. "It's cold but lovely and refreshing." As she withdrew her foot, Mr Mortimer, with a roguish grin, reached over and pushed her in backwards with a short laugh. It was only foolish fun, and as Margaret rose to the surface spluttering and laughing, she swam to the side. Leaning over, she caught hold of the portly man's ankle and gave it a sudden jerk. He lost his balance and pitched headlong into the water over her. The splash that ensued sprayed the three people on the grassy pool verge.

Tony quickly followed the others in, and after about ten minutes of splashing and swimming, they all clambered out and lay full-length on the sweet-scented turf.

For the first time, Roma Beaumont spoke. "As I expect you all know," she started, "Mrs Guyate here has very definite views on spiritualism." She paused and looked at each of the faces around her in turn, noting the effect her next statement would have upon her listeners.

"I am a medium," she said, dropping her dark eyes to her placidly clasped hands in her lap. "Tonight I want your assistance – all of you." She made a slight gesture with her arm, "I intend to hold a séance in the library."

The last word made Margaret visibly stiffen, she suddenly felt rather cold and somewhat uneasy.

With an unexpected flicker of electric lightning, followed by a deafening crash of thunder, high drops of drenching rain fell sizzling and hissing onto the dry ground.

For a moment nobody moved. Then another flash of lightning and a terrible clap of thunder seemed to split the very heavens apart. They gathered up their things and hurried towards the house to face the dreadful confinement of terror that hung over them like the menacing black clouds that had suddenly appeared in the sky.

A gust of hot wind enveloped them before they had reached the shelter of the house. They trooped inside, and closed the door on the angry weather, but could not shut out the cold, grasping fingers of fate that held them tightly within its terrible clutches. Although they did not understand the ominous double meaning, they knew that the storm had just begun.

7

Suspicion Arises

Dinner at *Wuthering Winds* that night was a quiet affair. That is to say, it was quiet inside the manor, but the summer storm had risen to a sort of fanatical fury outside, as though it was being deprived of its pleasure in tormenting human beings. The wind savagely whistled round the structure of the old house and prodigal bursts of rain beat fiercely at the latticed windows. The fiery streaks of lightning stabbed through the gathering gloom, and cast weird distorted shadows on the red brick walls and the lichen covered roof with its tall chimneys and jutting gables.

Skeels had moved swiftly and silently round the interior of the house, shutting windows and closing the green shutters that hung insecurely on their rust corroded hinges. The flashes of forked lightning fought a losing battle with the advancing darkness as the dusk closed about the house of mystery once more.

That this one-time old manor was a house of mystery, was known for miles around. Many a stormy winter's night, when the familiar company gathered round the blazing log fire that roared up the wide old-fashioned chimney of the *Cackling Hen*, would one of the inhabitants of Haywards Hill tell the story of the apparition that he had seen wandering aimlessly around the walls of *Wuthering Winds*.

James Barlow, who had the neat newspaper shop, had seen it. As had Joe Wiggens, the station master of Little Barlow, which was four miles away. The manor lay between Little Barlow and Haywards Hill, both tiny country villages, nestled among fields and woods and shut off from the rest of England by the confines of Ashdown Forest. It was further isolated from the world by the mighty barrier of grass-covered, chalk hills stretching from Sussex right through Hertfordshire. Sheltering at the foot of the steep slopes were dozens of typical Sussex villages and hamlets, rather similar to the one which boasted the *Cackling Hen*.

The facts concerning the embalming of Doctor Guyate were common knowledge in both villages and were often the topic for enthralling conversation between the local population. Some had even been heard to say that, "the doctor wern't dead at all but had a dummy made of hisself to make out that he were."

This statement was backed up by the tale of the village constable who had seen a figure wandering round outside the walls as though he was looking for a way in. How could the word of the law be doubted? He was tall and powerful, had a little beard and was shrouded up in a great raincoat and low brimmed hat.

Others murmured of bogeys and hobgoblins, or spirits and the devil. But, although the subject had been argued and discussed from end to end in both villages, no solution had ever been found, and no answer for their wandering minds had ever been given.

Most of the information that came from *Wuthering Winds* was supplied by the respectable servants. So, it was that Mr Skeels, the invaluable butler, who moved softly and discreetly round the candle-lit dinner table, with ears fully alert for any morsel of conversation that might be let to slip. Although he was never a chatterbox or a busybody, Mr Skeels liked to be well up in the affairs of all the occupants of the house, whether they were guests or not. Although he did not mix much with the villagers, a word or two dropped to Mrs Berkley was often the subject of a conversation among the ordinary people of the district.

However, what Mr Skeels did not know was the fact that he was being watched. His movements were observed with keen interest by both Margaret and Antony, their reasons clear to anyone who had over-heard the brief exchange between the two young guests at *Wuthering Winds*.

As they walked down the long hall to the oak panelled dining-room, Margaret had kept close to Tony, resting her hand on his strong arm. Tony felt a thrill of pride and happiness – he would even say love. Tenderly, he had leaned down to her and softly asked her how she fared.

Margaret had whispered back, "I am sure that the drawers of my room have been disturbed!"

Tony realised that something was very wrong. As the flicker of lightning lit up in bold outlines the objects in the passage, he knew that he had not been mistaken. The subsequent crash of thunder seemed to echo his re-alisation, causing him to flinch as if struck by an unseen force.

A rush of clarity overwhelmed him like a torrential flood. From his first moments of his stay here, he had felt a palpable unease. The grand, old house had an uncanny, mysterious atmosphere. The formidable presence of Miss Beaumont, the unbending politeness of the butler, Wilbur Mortimer's oddly jovial demeanour – so out of step with the setting – the talkative servants, and even his kindly aunt's absentminded eccentricity all appeared to be layers of deception. Everything around him felt disjointed, surreal and contrived.

Something was being hidden from him and Margaret – he was certain of it. *Perhaps*, he thought, *Roma Beaumont's seance would throw some light on the murkiness surrounding the secret of this place.*

He too had noticed that something in his room had been disturbed. Although he couldn't pinpoint exactly what was amiss, he felt as if someone had been there before him. This sensation best captured the vague, unsettling feeling that had lingered in his mind ever since.

But why, he wondered, *would anyone want to search his belongings, he had nothing to hide.*

Then, with a sickening fear gnawing at his heart, his grip tightening on Margaret's arm. He realised the reason for the searching of his room. He had nothing to hide, but someone else had! Somebody in this house was afraid of him! Someone harboured a secret crucial to their own well-being.

As they entered the dining room, Tony glanced at the people gathered in various postures around the long table. The two sets of silver candlesticks held tall, dripping candles that sent their flickering illuminations around the room, making the faces of the guests white and expressionless against the background of panelled walls.

Tony noticed that another person was in the room, other than his aunt, Skeels, Mortimer, Margaret and Miss Beaumont. It was Jenny Walker, the slight house-maid. She was putting the finishing touches to the table, and as Tony entered, she looked up.

Tony noticed that she had two pink spots of colour on either cheek, and with her starched, white apron and cap, he thought that she looked rather pretty.

As he stood in the doorway, she came towards him carrying a small wooden tray. He turned sideways to let her pass, but with a few quick steps, she drew level with him and pushed past. As she slipped by, hardly noticed by the other people in the room, Tony felt some-thing small, hard and square in shape pressed into his hand. He glanced down to see the piquant face of the girl looking up at him with an expression that instantly conveyed to him to be silent and pretend to have not noticed her.

Tony only had time to see that he was holding a small piece of paper, folded again and again, until it was a solid square. Evidently, the girl didn't want him to open it in front of the others, so he dropped it casually into his trouser pocket. He wondered vaguely for a minute whether it had anything to do with the track of his former thoughts. However, his aunt called him to sit down as they were starting dinner, so he dismissed the subject from his mind.

He took his seat next to Margaret. Skeels started serving dinner, unperturbed by the commotion outside, maintaining his customary calm and dignity. Mr Wilbur Mortimer was engaged in a lively conversation with Miss Roma Beaumont. He was asking the dark woman, who was dressed in a navy blue, slim fitting dress slashed with a peculiar Chinese pattern of gold and scarlet, about her intended séance. She had let her hair down so that it hung onto her shoulders in long black tresses that shone in the candlelight.

Margaret turned her head quickly as Mr Mortimer was heard to remark, "Let's hope this storm won't spoil the séance after dinner, folks," to the room in general, as was his curious habit. He glanced rather hard at Roma Beaumont before continuing, "This row won't make any difference, I hope?"

"No," Roma answered quickly, and then as though considering the situation, "on the contrary, atmospheric conditions like these are often of great assistance to a medium endeavouring to communicate with those who have passed over. I am expecting great results tonight."

Tony and Margaret, on the right of their hostess, distinctly heard her draw her breath in sharply. Evidently, Skeels heard it too, as he uncharacteristically set down the plates he was holding on the sideboard, with a clatter. All conversation stopped as everyone looked at him clenching his fists at his sides. He appeared to have an expression of defiance on his usually placid features. When he spoke, his voice sounded husky and strained.

"Ladies and Gentlemen," he began ceremoniously, "although as a rule I do not listen to your conversations, I cannot help but overhear what you say while I am present in the room with you."

Strangely enough, both Margaret and Tony noticed that he seemed to be keeping his eyes averted from his mistress' face. He was speaking with a dull precision, as though he had learnt the speech by heart.

"However," he went on, "having unintentionally overheard you express your intention of holding a séance after dinner, I would like to draw your attention to the condition of Mrs Guyate's heart, and under the circumstances, may I ask you to postpone your amusements to another night at least?" He indicated the window with his right hand, meaning that, above all, this particular night was liable to wreak havoc with his employer's physical and mental condition.

"Silence Skeels!" the words cut like a lash. Skeels recoiled a step. Roma Beaumont was on her feet, the chair fell backwards behind her with a crash.

"How dare you interfere with your superior's business! We are not amusing ourselves, and your opinions are not required." She raised her hand and pointed a slender white hand at the door. "Leave the room at once, and do not return until you are summoned."

Skeels' face was a mask of hate. He stood defiant, his whole countenance distorted with rage. For a moment or so, it looked like Skeels would be capable of throwing himself upon the tall, straight figure of the infuriated Roma Beaumont. His complexion had turned a ghastly yellow hue, the pulse on his forehead could plainly be seen beating with a palpating regularity as he clenched and unclenched his fists.

Gone was the discreet and dignified Skeels, once a seamless part of *Wuthering Winds*. In his place stood a ferocious figure, baring yellow fangs in a display of pent-up emotional rage that seemed to surge through his lean frame.

Slowly he started moving, but not towards the door. With his carefully cultured fingernails protruding like claws, he advanced on Roma Beaumont with beads of sweat on his brow glistening in the candlelight.

Margaret sat frozen in terror, while Tony, equally horrified, remained utterly motionless. Wilbur, stunned by the unexpectedness of the whole affair, only watched with raising alarm. With his body crouched and bent as though about to spring, Skeels did indeed look like a dreadful animal.

Roma Beaumont did not move. Even at that terrible, critical moment, the spectators to the ghastly scene were compelled to admire her courageous calmness.

Suddenly, the intolerable tension of the moment was broken by the quiet, tremored voice of the mistress and owner of the old manor. "I am sure Skeels was only thinking of me, I think I understand."

Like oil poured on troubled waters, the tension and strain seemed to diminish. Gradually, with a murmured threat, the man's violent manner dropped like a discarded cloak, and still fixing Roma with his baleful eyes, he withdrew from the room.

A second later, the door shut with a deafening bang that left the echoes mingling with the rumbling skies outside.

8

The Séance

The party of people entered the shadowy and sombre library of *Wuthering Winds*. Mrs Lucile Guyate led the way carrying a long candlestick with a solitary flickering candle, casting its feeble light onto the dark oak panels. The door swung open with an eerie creak as they pushed it from the outside. The sound seemed to Margaret to be magnified in volume during the short break in the monotonous crashes of thunder and the vivid flashes of lightning.

In here, the curtains of heavy material cloaked the large glass doors that opened out onto the lawn at the south of the house. The whole room, for the greater part of the day, was completely devoid of sunlight. The jutting gables and the curve of the structure leading to the west wing of the manor created an effective screen. A number of unused outhouses stood with their rotting overhead beams lending a strange charm and attraction to the estate.

Margaret was wide-eyed with nervous excitement, and with a tingling feeling up her spine, she set foot in the bleak room. She looked up at Tony; his lips were tightly compressed and his brow puckered. Roma Beaumont seemed to glide into the room, her tall figure casting a weird moving shape on the panels. She pushed the old-fashioned chairs into a semi-circle, a little distance from the cabinet, which contained the grisly relics that held the tragic memory of Mr Guyate's life. Lucile now placed the single candle on a low side table. While she had been holding it in her trembling hands it had reduced the light to a weak, trembling glow; now as it remained still, it radiated a warm illumination that penetrated to the furthermost corners of the room.

Margaret and Tony, standing arm-in-arm by the door, suddenly realised that Roma was speaking to them. Wilbur Mortimer sat further back from the others against the oak panels to the right of the coffin-shaped casket. Strangely enough for him, he did not move or speak during the whole séance.

"Will you all come and sit around in this circle?" Tony noticed that Roma Beaumont was speaking listlessly with a peculiarly flat tone compared to her usual pleasant voice.

Together, the two young people moved to the chairs and sat down. Lucile sat on the edge of a chair next to Margaret. Her face was white with strain and her eyes appeared to be two deep, dark sockets. A sudden roll of thunder filled the room with an ominous ringing crash, followed by a sharp tattoo on the latticed windows behind the thick curtains. The solitary candle wavered its feeble light. To Margaret it had the effect of making the room seem very big and dark. She looked up, except for the arc of light thrown by the candle, the rest of the ceiling was completely obscured with gloom.

Margaret shivered slightly. Tony realised that her hand was suddenly chilly and damp with nervous perspiration. He felt a tremor take her as she shivered. He noticed with interest that the dark woman was letting down her glinting black hair. It was falling onto her slim shoulders in coils, shining with electricity. She closed her eyes and clasped her hands behind her back, and then in a low chanting voice, she began to recite. Her slim, curved body swayed to and fro in rhythm to the metre of her words. Tony could hardly fathom the change – one moment a moderately young, possibly attractive woman, the next a chanting, swaying creature, like a medieval witch.

Moving slowly, with a poise in keeping with her murmuring, she commenced to move to the large French windows. Margaret noticed that the air of the dim room seemed filled with a deep, low, throbbing sound, like the pounding of many drums. The noise seemed to fill her ears with a relentless beating. She did not realise that the blood coursing excitedly through her veins was sending pulses to her head.

Tony sat spellbound. Although he had never had any belief in spiritualism, he could not deny that some strange force appeared to be at work in the old library of *Wuthering Winds*. He looked across to his aunt who was sitting very straight and upright in her chair, clasping her white hands together fiercely, showing the knuckles up clearly in the ghostly, pale candlelight. Wilbur Mortimer did not move.

Roma Beaumont had reached the doors and was standing in front of them. They saw her put out her hands and take hold of the thick curtains.

The glass covered casket containing the body of Dr. Guyate showed up its eerie outline against the dark panels; the circle of people drawn around enclosed the embalmed figure entirely.

With a sudden, quick pull, Roma Beaumont flung back the drapings at the windows. Seizing the brass handle, she flung open the doors. A rush of cold air enveloped the room. Margaret and Tony felt the damp rain blow in a tiny spray onto their faces. Roma Beaumont remained there in the open doorway. Then, with slow, faltering steps she turned and moved across the room to Lucile Guyate.

The night seemed to be suddenly calm now. Only a gentle sound penetrated the clear air, the noise of softly swaying trees brushing their leaves in the night wind.

Roma Beaumont stood in front of Lucile Guyate, her voice was low and deep, "Now you must unlock the cabinet." The words seemed to have a paralysing effect upon the owner of the old manor.

Tony watched his aunt sitting taunt and tense on the edge of the chair as she gazed into the other woman's eyes. For several seconds she did not move, and then very slowly she rose. She was holding a small golden key. Funny he had not noticed it before.

She walked unsteadily towards the cabinet that contained the dead body of her husband. She stopped and stood peering through the glass panel into the casket. Her figure obscured Margaret and Tony's view. Only Wilbur Mortimer saw her stretch out a trembling hand towards the keyhole. She was pointing the key at the lock.

Tony and Margaret heard a faint click and then a quiet creak. Mrs Guyate stepped back and sat down sharply, still keeping her eyes fixed on the object of everyone's attention – the embalmed body.

Oh, the horror! The cabinet stood open! A faint, sweet, sickly odour reached out into the room. The white shirt front on the figure glowed dully in the flickering candlelight.

The protruding grey beard and piercing eyes seemed to be alive! Margaret felt weak with nervous fear. To kill the illusion of life in the body she was forced to divert her eyes for a second.

Roma Beaumont was once again moving towards the glass doors standing open to the night. She stood still in the doorway looking up at the sky at the low-hanging storm clouds. Slowly she raised her arms and extended the fingers of her hands above her head.

For some seconds she stood poised, and then with a sudden, unexpected cry she screamed into the dark night, waving her arms about in the air, swaying her body to and fro. "Doctor Herbert Guyate, I summon you to retake possession of your earthly body, to communicate with your earthly wife, who awaits below the coming of your message! By your fathers' forefathers, by the power which conceives men in the womb of women, I appeal to you to return to the earth where you once lived!"

With a flash of lightning, followed immediately by a clash of thunder, the heavy oak doors behind the group of spellbound people, flung open with a violent crash.

Everyone in the room jumped with fright and spun around. The figure of a man stood framed in the doorway – a man wild-eyed and white of countenance, with his hair ruffled and his black suit clinging to him with dampness. It was the usually immaculate figure of Skeels, the butler of *Wuthering Winds*. Immobilised by dread, they watched him stagger across the room into the centre of the circle of people.

Drinking in the scene at a glance, he sank on his knees before his distressed mistress. He buried his head in her lap, and with a faint moan, remained in this position for several moments before raising his head. With a face working with fear, he blurted out the barely audible sentence, "Oh ma'am... dead... Oh ma'am..."

Suddenly to everyone's surprise, the voice of the tubby American cut in on Skeels' speech. "Who is dead? Explain yourself, man!"

Tony noted a distinct note of authority and command behind the usually placid voice of Wilbur Mortimer.

"It's her," gasped the butler, pointing out at the French windows. "Jenny Walker, the housemaid – lying dead out on the veranda by the back door."

An ominous flash of lightning, and a roll of thunder gave emphasis to the ghastly statement. A gust of wind made the single candle flicker before it finally expired.

The nauseating fear of death crept up through the uneven floorboards and enveloped the terror-stricken people in the room. Darkness closed in on them.

9

Fear's Deadly Grip

The storm had abated slightly but showed every sign of resuming the momentum of its former fury. The moon had broken through the black clouds and sailed like a stately galleon on a stormy sea.

The two young guests at the manor faced each other across the drawing room. "Where is she?" Margaret's question was spontaneous.

"We have laid her in her room."

"*Is* she dead?" faltered Margaret, grabbing Tony's hand.

"Yes."

"How? Why?" beseeched Margaret.

"Her face is horribly distorted, but as far as we can see, there are no marks indicating physical violence." Tony moved to the sideboard and poured a couple of stiff whiskey and sodas.

With hardly a sound, the door swung open and Wilbur Mortimer stood in the doorway. His face was white and perplexed but he had assumed an entirely different bearing to the mood that had been his most marked characteristic before. "The others will be down shortly. Something has got to be done about this affair. We have got to come to some conclusion and decide just how the maid met her – er – death," he stammered.

Tony noticed how he had faltered on the last word, and glanced at Margaret before he spoke the ominous word. *Death*. Tony turned the word over in his mind. There was something dreadfully suggestive and terrible about those five letters.

Margaret felt her mind was numb. She found it difficult to concentrate and found herself moving unconsciously nearer to Tony. At the back of her mind was a voice telling her, *Watch Wilbur Mortimer*. Vaguely she had a feeling that the American was more than he wanted people to think he was. *Is this what they call womens' intuition?* she wondered.

The three people heard footsteps outside the door. Mrs Lucile Guyate and Roma Beaumont entered the room followed by the tight-lipped Skeels; all of them looked strained and tense. Mrs Guyate sat down heavily in a deep armchair. Margaret noticed how she suddenly appeared to look much older than her first impression had led her to believe.

For several seconds, the assorted individuals scattered around the room looked at each other in silence. Tony felt the discomfort mounting. He felt rather than saw the striking black eyes of Roma Beaumont boring into him. Skeels in turn, standing a step back from the group, was a striking figure directing his silent hate at the dark woman.

Margaret felt the strings of her strained nerves tighten as she watched the little old lady sitting in front of her, fidgeting with her hands. Her face was a grey, ashen hue and faint, blue lines surrounded her mouth and eyes. She guessed at the anxiety of the lonely widow of the manor, now shrouded in mystery and fear. Wilbur Mortimer's face was an immovable mask; as she looked across to his profile, she felt again the pang that had stirred her before.

It was evident that the events of the last hour and a half had begun to tell on all of the inhabitants of the old manor. Tony was the first to break the silence. "Let's all have a drink."

He moved across the room and filled his and Margaret's glasses as well as four others. Automatically, he handed them round and the last one he gave to Skeels, who accepted it and swallowed the contents in one gulp. Tony wondered if he drank much. He certainly had plenty of opportunity and access to drink a large quantity of liquor. From what he had seen there was always a good stock kept in the house.

He suddenly realised that he had been doing the job that Skeels would normally have done under almost any other circumstances – handing round the drinks. *Strange,* he thought, *how quickly convention is forgotten when the mind is preoccupied.*

Wilbur Mortimer spoke up, "The first thing that we must do is find out just how the maid died. She was young and therefore it is doubtful that she was suffering from any disease that might be likely to strike her down at any time." He glanced meaningfully at Lucile Guyate.

Both Margaret and Tony noticed immediately how very un-American this statement sounded. Wilbur Mortimer seemed to notice it too, for he hastened to add, "Well folks, Marshton and I couldn't see any visible signs of violence as we carried her upstairs."

Tony felt a moment of deep resentment of Wilbur Mortimer's familiarity. Mrs Lucile Guyate shuddered visibly and Margaret impulsively walked over to her. She perched on the arm of the chair, placed her arm lightly along the back, with her hand resting gently on the shoulder of Tony's aunt. The older woman turned her head and Margaret was pleased to see just the flicker of a smile playing on her lips.

Tony looked hard at Skeels before asking in a quiet, firm voice, "Did you move anything prior to your calling us, and are you sure that – er – she was – er – dead?"

Skeels allowed himself to consider the question before replying. "No, Mr Anthony." He spoke in a low voice with a definite note of respect. Gone was the defiant and fierce-looking Skeels who had caused such a stir just after dinner. In his place, was the usual discreet and submissive butler. Now looking white and a little frightened, but nevertheless, still a perfect, confidential, old family retainer. That he was devoted to his aunt, Tony was certain. His concern was for his mistress, and what was more, Tony was glad that Skeels had endeavoured to protect his aunt's health and wellbeing, particularly from the weird schemings of Miss Beaumont. As Tony watched Skeels now, he knew that a deep-rooted hatred for the dark, professed medium lay beneath the docile manner of the butler's character.

"I did not move anything at all. I just stood and gazed at poor Jenny Walker for a minute. I was too shocked to do anything! Of course, I wasn't sure that she was dead, but when I saw her lying there with the rain beating down on her in that pool of water, with a ghastly expression on her face – which I saw clearly during the flashes of the lightning – I never doubted for a second that she was." Skeels faltered on the last word and turned his face away, muttering to himself, "Horrible, horrible."

Then once again, in the same low voice, "I shall never be able to forget the sight of her. Whatever caused it. Never." The wretched man winced and broke off, taking a step backwards and standing with a bowed head near the door.

Margaret listened with the others in silence. She was sorry for Skeels, she had a feeling that he was perfectly genuine. In all the detective stories that she had ever read, it was always the person one least suspected that was the murderer – she cut her thoughts short. *Murder!* What had made her think of murder? Because a maid had died in the middle of a storm, she immediately dramatised the situation and thought of murder. In her pent-up state of nervousness, she suddenly felt she wanted to laugh.

The harsh, discordant noise erupted in the silent room, startling everyone. No one moved; no one spoke. Although it was clearly a laugh, its sudden, untimely nature jolted everyone, breaking through the intense focus of all six people present.

For one awful second, Margaret believed that she had allowed her self-control to relax, and that the strain on her nerves had snapped her reason, causing her to laugh with a mad, grating screech.

Then, every eye in the room turned to the dreadful figure who had uttered the ghastly sound. It was Roma Beaumont. She stood by the window, a fanatical gleam of triumph in her dark eyes. The array of steadily burning candles caught the lights in her long hair.

Margaret suddenly realised that Miss Beaumont had not rearranged it after the séance. The woman's white claw-like hand was raised in a gesture of pride above her head. The long, clinging gown shimmered with the graceful movement of her body. The voice had a distinct ring of satisfaction in it.

"It worked!" she cried, throwing out her arms. "He has answered my summons!" The occupants of the room stood transfixed. "The girl was psychic," she went on, her voice rising to a high note of hysteria. "She saw the spirit of Dr. Guyate returning to occupy his earthly body!" Again that dreadful laugh, striking a chill in the hearts of the onlookers.

With a wide gesture of her long, bare arms and trembling hands she shrieked, "She died of shock! The spirit of Doctor Herbert Guyate has reoccupied his body and is here, in this old house!"

The peals of fiendish and gloating laughter awoke the echoes of the manor house and continued until the horrible sound was reclaimed and died on the stormy night air.

10
Night of Terror

"The night will be short even if it seems long," repeated Margaret to herself as she lay in the high four-postered bed. The darkness was heavy about her and the rain beating on the latticed windows gave her an uncanny feeling of fear that she struggled to quell.

Tony's comforting few words, as she stood with him by the door to her room, kept returning to her mind. "Everything will come out all right, trust me." And then a pause, "My darling." She had heard how husky his voice had sounded.

My darling. She allowed her thoughts to cling to the words, and then from somewhere down below she heard a whirring sound, followed by a deep resounding clang. With her hands gripping the sheets until the knuckles showed white, she realised that she had merely heard the great grandfather clock downstairs striking one o'clock.

She sank back on the pillow, only to start up again as a vivid flash of lightning reached its penetrating light through the uncurtained windows. Clearly, she saw the panelled walls and the few articles of furniture that stood about the room. The ancient hangings, above the head of the bed, cast her in shadow for the brief second that the light ruled the darkness. Then came the rolling crash of thunder echoing through the old house, filling the rooms and passages with the vibrating voice of the elements, raised as if in anger at this land of selfish men.

Margaret turned over and tried to sleep, but she could not. Her mind was heavy and drugged with the terror that had hit her so unexpectedly. She tried to turn her thoughts to those ridiculous symbols that are so fool-ishly believed to invite deep and restful slumber. She refrained from counting sheep from sheer obstinacy. Instead, she tried to think of someone who had quite quickly become very dear to her...

But her thoughts were hardly under her own control any more. If only she could sleep. She tried to think of colours – anything to make her sleep! Such silly things... *My darling* – deep purple came to mind. Jenny Walker, the maid lying out in the rain – bright red. A field of sheep, she tried to stop herself. And yet she was counting.

One, two, three... slowly and drowsily, with a feeling of blankness consuming her whole mind and thoughts, she was counting... four, five, six. Counting, nothing in particular, just forming the numbers in her mind. Seven, eight, nine... and yet something was rhythmically propelling her thoughts along, sweeping her forward, holding her spellbound, forcing her to count... ten. Margaret sat up with a start.

For just a second, her mind failed to function. She was vividly aware of a tingling feeling in her hair and her tongue seemed to cleave to the roof of her mouth. Then, with hot blood rushing in a torrent to her head, and a dreadful numbness binding her body to inactivity, she realised what it was that she had actually been counting.

Quiet and muffled, but distinct enough to a sensitive ear, she heard footsteps! Footsteps coming along the passage towards her door. Every sense in her screamed for her to cry out aloud, but she was unable to do more than open her mouth and utter a tiny hoarse gurgle.

There was something foreboding about the footsteps. Something ghastly and terrifying. Why should footsteps in the night have this strange effect? Why should it not be merely one of the guests or servants passing along the passage? Why should she have this absurd feeling, this uncanny suspicion? Margaret could not tell.

The whole incident might just be a perfectly normal occurrence boosted by her overwrought nerves and fertile imagination. And yet, why were the sounds so faint, so obviously intended to be silent? Why did she feel such a horrible psychological connection between these footsteps in the night and the strange unexplained passing of the young housemaid?

Above all, why should anyone walk along the passage, unlit and eerie as it was, at the dead of night or rather the early hours of the morning? Margaret knew instinctively that the night had passed long before. Was it not late when she had gone to bed, when she had stood at the door with Tony?

His name cut in upon her thoughts. Where was he now? Perhaps this was him coming to her now! Her heart leapt within her at the thought, but the next second she knew instinctively that it was not him.

The footfalls came nearer. The moon, for a fleeting second, broke through the heavy, low clouds which had until now, obscured the radiant beams from sending their ghostly pale light to this earth of men. Margaret saw the door become vividly illuminated. She noticed the stout, oak panelling studded with strong iron bolts and the circular ring of metal near the side, hanging like a noose. *Horrible thought!* Yet the footsteps came on.

Petrified and paralysed, Margaret could do nothing but stare. Stare into that muscular door, trying to pierce the depths of wood that separated her from the barely audible creator of the measured tread.

She heard the silent step stop. She stared and then started to sob. Soundlessly, her breath came in violent, choking gasps.

The pale moon cast its last weird shadow onto the walls of the old house through the lattice window of Margaret's horror-filled bedroom, then with a last desperate glimmer, withdrew and cowered behind sodden clouds. For a second, there was silence.

Margaret held her breath. She felt an insane desire to shriek out, *Come in, you coward, let me see your terrible form!* For in her intense dread, she had formed the uncanny belief that the object that stood just beyond her room was from another world. The effects of Roma Beaumont's hysterical performance were having a powerful bearing on her imaginative character, and coupled with the strange and unprovoked death of Jenny Walker, her mind was in a turmoil.

Then once again, the same rhythmic step, quiet and nondescript, commenced to tread its almost noiseless way past her door.

Margaret collapsed weakly back on the billowy, white pillow. She rested her hand across her delicately rounded breasts and felt the pounding of her panic-stricken heart through the flimsiness of her pretty nightgown. Who or what had stood for those ghastly seconds in the old, stone passage of this house of enigma and unease?

Slowly, she felt the power of movement returning to her seemingly lifeless body. Gradually, she sat up. She was consumed with an overwhelming curiosity to investigate the movements of this sinister, lurking prowler.

She slipped her legs out from the coverings on the bed. She felt the chilled night air sweep across the room from under the heavy door. With her long hair streaming onto her slim shoulders, she moved softly to the door. A sudden rattle of driving rain, yet again rapped on the glass window panes, making her pull up sharply. Her hand showed white and gleaming in the darkness, outstretched towards the door handle.

She gripped the ring and turned it away from her. She heard the click as the latch was raised. Then, clearly and loudly, came the blatant noise of a hard tap, as of human knuckles on wood. Once, twice... the rapping sound was distinct and harsh in the silence of the old manor. Outside the elements added their jostling chaos to the nerve-racking atmosphere.

All at once, came the patter of running feet. The muffled, light thud of swiftly moving footsteps returning back down the passage, making Margaret's blood freeze once more. She stood motionless. *Would it come in? Would it pass? Would it stop? Was it real? Was it human? What was it?* The thoughts came in a swift rush to her overtaxed brain.

"Oh, my god!" Scarcely knowing what she was doing, she stumbled forward. She felt trapped! Anything to get out and get away. Throwing her weight backwards, she flung open the door. She felt the rush of air as a large, dark, swiftly moving object flashed by her along the corridor.

The soft echo of the creaking door was dying in the silence of the heavily carpeted corridor. Silent it was, except for the pattering sound of quick footsteps.

With one step forward, she would see who it was, or what it was, that had walked in the hush of the early morning to rap twice upon the panels of the passage. One step, and a revelation would take place. A turn of her head and her terror would become a thing of empty humour, or it might increase to gigantic proportions and all the unfounded, unbased horror of her distracted mind would sum up before her that dreadful vision of, she knew not what.

With a resolute stride, causing her gown to billow behind her like pale pink wings, she was on the landing. Yet another stride, and her hands gripped the bannister rail in a feverish clasp. For a split second, she stood frozen. Then, as a wave of feminine fear and helplessness washed over her, consuming her very soul, she turned her head and stared down the passage where the source of her terror had retreated.

At first, she could see nothing. Unsettling, eerie shadows engulfed her tortured eyes within its realms. Then, like a stabbing finger of light, accusing and fearsome, a flash of forked lightning ran across the darkened skies and cut its forcible way through the long, thin latticed windows of the old house and cast a spotlight of illumination upon the object of Margaret's attention. Clearly, she saw it. Distinctly, she recognised it. There was no mistaking that upright, thick-set figure, with the whiteness of the shirtfront showing up in the split second brilliance of the lightning flash. The little, grey beard and sharp forcible features made an immemorial profile. It was the figure from the casket in the library – Herbert Guyate.

The lightning died and the blackness closed upon the slim, lightly clad girl who stood staring, mortified and numb, with a great, overwhelming terror that hung in the air around her. The wind howled with a low, mournful noise around the skirting of *Wuthering Winds*. The black thunderclouds, obscuring the moon again, lent a terrible, menacing air to the storm-shocked night. High up on the landing of the third floor, stood the terrified Margaret. She felt the atmosphere of storm and tension but she saw and heard nothing.

Below her was a dreadful vision, rising up out of the blankness of the stupefied mind. It was the face of the manor's terror. Although she could no longer see the awful features, they appeared to be before her eyes as a mirage. It seemed that nothing could break the spell of those last few ghastly seconds, passing with a flash in the night.

A stair creaked with the pressure of a descending foot. Margaret finally released the overpowering horror that had gripped her like iron. She opened her mouth and let out a loud, piercing scream, unleashing all the pent-up terror that filled her heart, mind, soul, and very being.

The rolling, growing claps of ominous thunder rose with a mighty fanatical fury, buffeting the noise backwards and forwards inside the building and completely hiding the silent thump as Margaret, overwhelmed, slumped to the floor.

Pattering footfalls passed down the stairs and descended to the ground level. The thunder ceased, while the still figure lay across the landing with a halo of hair flowing onto the carpet. A slim, pale arm outstretched across the passage with a tightly clenched hand portraying a complete consumption of fear. The air was heavy, the darkness was thick. Silence descended again.

With a crash that echoed through the old house, the door to Anthony Marshton's room was flung open. The next second, he emerged from the room, dressed in his blue striped pyjamas, with his hair tousled, and a look of alertness upon his face.

He strode along the passage but he had barely got far before the door to the right opened. Tony was surprised to see Wilbur Mortimer, fully clothed, and holding an electric torch!

"What in hell's name was that?"declared the American, flashing his light along the corridor.

"How the devil should I know," barked Tony in return. He broke off suddenly, catching sight of the still, white figure sprawled across the landing past the main staircase.

"My god, it's Margaret!" he exclaimed, pointing a finger towards the prostrate girl. With a few rapid strides, the two men were beside Margaret, lifting her gently and patting her cold hands and face.

Meanwhile, another door opened further along the wide corridor to the right of the large shallow staircase. Roma Beaumont, dressed in a long, red dressing gown, appeared in the door of her room. The wide sleeves of her gown fluttered as she made her way towards the group of people along the landing passage. She stopped short as she saw the focus of the two men's attention.

"My god!" Her face was a white mask and her dark eyes burned with what Tony thought afterwards to be a look almost of fear. "Has he killed her?"

Wilbur glanced up quickly. "Who?"

Tony reassured, "No, she'll be alright in a minute, I think."

Ignoring the others, he slipped his hands under Margaret and picked her up. She lay in his arms, close to his body. Her beautiful hair falling in soft wavy coils with the graceful lines of her lithe body curving into his eager, young arms. He held her pale, unturned face to his shoulder.

They approached Margaret's room and Tony stepped back while Wilbur did an inspection with the beam of his torch. They then entered the room together with Roma Beaumont following close behind.

Very gently, Tony laid the unconscious girl on the crumbled sheets on the big bed. Fumbling on the table by the side of it, he picked up a box of matches and lit the candle.

With a steady flicker, the candle bathed the room in a dim, amber light. Margaret stirred and opened her eyes. For some seconds she lay still and then with a violent start, she sat up suddenly. Clutching, with a frantic, fearful grip onto the sleeve of Tony's pyjama jacket, and staring with a dreadful fixed gaze straight ahead, she opened her mouth and tried to speak.

At first her lips moved soundlessly and then in a tiny whisper she gasped, "Has it gone?"

She then seemed to become aware of the group of people around her, and with a sigh of relief, she sank back onto the pillow, still holding Tony's arm.

"What was it?" asked Wilbur Mortimer tensely.

For a full minute there was dead silence. Margaret looked from face to face while they waited expectantly for her to answer. When she finally spoke, the effect upon the listeners was curiously mixed.

"It was Doctor Herbert Guyate," she whispered.

Tony gasped and his eyes earnestly sought the girl's face. Roma Beaumont recoiled a step and gave a deep sigh. But Wilbur Mortimer stood up suddenly, and with a last hard look at Margaret, he strode from the room.

The others silently watched him go. He went with the air of a man with a definite purpose. He had one, and the others knew it. But what it was, other than the fact that it centred around Margaret's extraordinary disclosure, they were at a loss to know.

Margaret, now almost fully recovered, but still keeping her hold on Tony's arm, spoke again. "Didn't either of you hear it too?" she enquired, gazing earnestly from face to face.

Roma Beaumont moved round the tall bed and came and sat down on the side of it. She looked intently at Margaret before asking, "What was it, dear?"

To Tony, that last word grated horribly.

"I heard footsteps and then a loud tapping noise," shuddered Margaret. "I came out to see what it was and by the light of a flash of lightning, I saw a figure that I can swear was Doctor Guyate." She broke off and put her hands over her face. "It was awful, awful!"

Very gently, Tony placed his arm about her shoulders. "I heard a tapping too, I think," he announced.

"So did I," said Roma decidedly. "But I didn't know what it was."

"I must go and see my aunt," said Tony with a flash of inspiration and stood up.

Margaret clutched his arm, "I'll come with you." The silent look in her eyes spoke volumes to Tony.

All together, they proceeded back along the landing to the door of Lucile Guyate's room. Tony knocked lightly on the panels. There was no answer! He tried again, harder this time. Then he banged with his clenched fist. For a moment they waited. He seized the door ring and turning it, he pushed the door sharply inwards. The darkness met them like a wall.

"Go back and get that candle, would you?" Tony asked Miss Beaumont.

Margaret watched her unfaltering footsteps from behind. It was more than she would have cared to do, to return to that room by herself. Yet the other woman had not even hesitated.

In a few seconds the tall dark woman reappeared, this time carrying the candle which shed its glowing rays onto the polished woodwork and oak panelling of the passage. She handed it to Tony, who took it with a steady hand, and together they entered the room.

Margaret glanced quickly about; it was as barely furnished as her room. All the pieces of furniture were old and wooden. The bed was the same four-posted, enormous structure that seemed to be fitted in all the bedrooms. The window was curtained, but the sound of the driving rain on the latticed window pane was heard by all three of them. But it was the figure on the bed that attracted their unwilling attention.

Now, Lucile Guyate, the owner of *Wuthering Winds,* lay coiled in a pose of terror upon the dishevelled sheets. Her fingers, fully extended from her hands, and the expression of panic portrayed on her pale face, told only too clearly the tale of dread that Margaret has previously related. Just what she had seen, they did not know, but the fact that she had been overcome by the hysteria of the moment was only too apparent.

What terrible secret lay behind this night's happenings? What strange apparition had Margaret seen from the landing? Why had Wilbur Mortimer rushed off in such a hurry when he had heard Margaret's amazing disclosure? Roma Beaumont was unafraid, why? In a wild jumble of thoughts all these things flashed through Anthony's confused mind while he stood gazing at the still figure of his elderly aunt. *What connection did the storm have to the figure on the stairs, the tapping sound and the death of the maid, to the strange mixture of characters thrown together by fate in this old house?*

In a heartbeat he was across the room bending over his aunt. Very faintly, he could hear her breathing. He knew she was in a bad way.

Without warning, another figure appeared framed in the doorway. Skeels, the trusty butler, held a candle in his right hand.

For a second, neither Tony nor Margaret recognised him. If Roma was surprised, she showed no sign. She stood impassive and calm. *Almost heedlessly callous,* thought Margaret.

"My aunt has had another of her attacks," said Tony shortly. He did not feel like going into details at that moment. *Who knows, Skeels might be able to throw some light upon the mystery. Strange servants do strange things in strange houses at strange times!*

Skeels was dressed in a long flower-covered dressing gown printed in a medley of bright colours. His side whiskers were standing out from his ashen face. The dark lines under his deep set eyes told Anthony that the butler had also had difficulty in resting after the dramatic events of the previous evening.

As Skeels crossed the room to the bedside, he shot Roma Beaumont a distrustful glance. He was evidently thinking that the tall, dignified woman, who professed to be a spiritualist medium, was the cause of all the dreadful misery. For a split second, Tony mused, perhaps she was.

Skeels turned and asserted, "There is very little any of you can do, I am afraid, but I have seen her in just such a state many times before. I think she will recover."

He paused to see if anyone would challenge his authoritative tone of speaking, but nobody did. They realised that Skeels was by far the most able person to deal with this fresh and dismal part of the dreadful proceedings. Had he not been attending to Mrs Guyate for more years than most of them could remember?

"Right, we had better go back to bed then," said Roma Beaumont abruptly.

"Perhaps you would tell me what the scream was that I heard? Also how was it that you came to find Mrs Guyate in this distressed condition?" inquired Skeels politely.

As briefly as possible, Tony explained. He saw no reason to withhold anything from this fine and faithful old man. Skeels listened attentively with a serious and strained face. Eventually he raised his head and said, "I think I will stay with Mrs Guyate; she might be glad to have me here when she recovers."

"Can I stay too, there might be something I can do to help," suggested Margaret.

"Thank you, Miss Palmer, but I think I can manage. It is only a matter of giving her some medicine, and I have done that so many times that I am quite used to it," replied Skeels, giving Margaret a warm smile of appreciation.

They left the room together. Tony, glancing back, saw the frail lady with the peculiar form of the devoted butler sitting beside her, gently patting her back as she lay on the big bed. It reminded him of an old picture he remembered as a boy, of the sheepdog, sitting beside the coffin of his dead master. He could remember that the picture was called *The Last Mourner*. With a tiny shudder, he softly closed the door behind him.

Just at that moment, a sound was heard down below. For one short second, the three of them stood frozen. Margaret took a step towards Tony and caught his arm. The corridor was dark and full of strange shadows. The beating fingers of the rain pattered relentlessly against the tall windows. They heard the sound of footsteps start to ascend the stairs. A flash of lightning cut across the hall.

"My god! It's coming back!" The crash of thunder merged with Margaret's frenzied words.

They heard the steady footsteps continue upwards. Their straining gaze perceived a dull glow rising from the stairs. Tony felt his spine tingle with a strange feeling of curiosity and terror. The light increased in volume. He felt the pressure of Margaret's grip upon his arm. That strange phantom light seemed to be flashing from side to side.

"It's Wilbur Mortimer with his torch," uttered Roma Beaumont in her confident way.

The revelation brought such a sudden feeling of relief to the other two as they realised the accuracy of the statement, that Margaret lurched heavily against Tony, who had a nauseating sensation fill his whole mind. For some seconds, the two young people were unable to move, and it was not until Wilbur's thick figure appeared above the line of the landing that Tony spoke. "Where the devil have you been walking around in the middle of the night?" he demanded.

The American looked surprised but he offered no explanation. Instead, he countered the question with another. "Did Mrs Guyate hear that tapping noise?"

"Yes," answered Tony. "Did you?"

The American nodded his head in assent, and reaching the top of the stairs suggested that they all retired to bed.

For one moment, tender-hearted Margaret became completely exasperated. "Don't you realise that Mrs Guyate is in a very bad state? She's had another heart attack and you talk about going to bed!"

Tony was relieved to see the unexpected look of understanding appear on the plump face of the short man. "Is there anything we can do?"

"No," Roma Beaumont cut in sharply. Then, more softly, "Nothing. Skeels is with her."

After a few more words, they split up. Roma went her way, Wilbur went his. As he walked back, flashing his torch along the ground, Tony saw by the feeble light that there was mud thickly caked upon his shoes.

As the American shut his door, closing off the last of the light, Margaret moved closer towards Anthony. In the flicker of lightning, Tony reached for Margaret's slender figure and said, "I'll see you to your room."

She seemed relieved. They walked slowly along the landing arm in arm. He opened the heavy, oak door and the glimmer of light from the rain-lashed window showed him where the washstand with another candle stood. He passed ahead and struck the match.

When he turned with the light behind him, he saw Margaret had closed the door and was leaning on it. She looked very young and beautiful with the soft pink shades of her nightdress illuminated in the dark.

He stood still, their eyes met and held. The night suddenly seemed to have become very quiet. He felt his heart go out to her, his pulse raced, and his love for this girl knew no bounds. Her very defencelessness and trusting sincerity gave fire to his young heart, mind and body!

Margaret returned his gaze steadily. Something within her told her that this was the man that she loved. She knew it would be dangerous to touch him and yet she wanted to so much. *Would it be wrong? This man's love was true love. It was pure and clean.*

The room would be very dark and frightening if not for him. Of the darkness, the night, the house, she was afraid. Of Tony – the love of her life – she was unafraid. With their hearts and minds in union, their love and passions in sync, nothing could keep them apart.

Acting simultaneously, they met in the centre of the room. Margaret buried her face in Anthony's shoulder.

He held her very tight. He looked down tenderly while she glanced up at him. A vivid flash of lightning flooded the room with a brilliant radiance as their lips touched.

Her soft, sweetly curved mouth, still wet from his kisses, smiled whimsically as she whispered, "Darling, I am afraid."

He held her at arm's length. "Of what?"

"Of – of –" she glanced down, "of being left alone."

He drew her to him and very gently picked her up. He leaned slightly sideways and blew out the candle. For some seconds he stood there. Her arms were around his neck, her tired, tousled head on his shoulder. His back was very straight and his heart beat very fast. The cloak of lovers' foolishness enveloped them.

"Darling, do you love me?"

She whispered, "Yes."

The slashing rain was to them like wild passionate music, the lightning as radiant as love, the thunder like the pounding of their hearts. The elements seemed to bring to them God's holy blessing. They waited to receive it and then felt it bestowed.

11

The First Glimpse

The rattle of an old Ford drawing upon the gravel of the drive made Margaret cross to her window and peer out. Down below, what seemed to be a nineteen twenty-five model, stood in front of the porch. It was Skeels' idea that Anthony and Wilbur should phone the garage eight miles up the Shoreham Road, and hire a car to spend the afternoon motoring into Eastbourne and back along the Upper Downs Road.

Both the men had been attracted by the idea and greeted it with enthusiasm. Margaret would have liked to have gone with them, but Tony had been implicit that only he and Wilbur should go. They both declared themselves expert drivers, having quite a long, friendly argument as to who would drive. Eventually they agreed to take it in turns.

The garage owner instructed one of his mechanics to drive it over directly after lunch and to cycle back to the garage. On their return, later in the evening, they were to phone again and then the garage owner himself would collect the car. Upon hearing that it was for *Wuthering Winds,* the proprietor declared himself *delighted to please the gentlemen.*

Margaret saw that the fawn-coloured car was a battered two-seater, and it had a large, closable rumble seat. This, when opened, could be a novel seating arrangement, or when closed, a large luggage carrier. The back was presently open, with a bicycle strapped to it. Margaret watched as the mechanic clambered out of the car, walk around to the rear and unstrap the bicycle. Then he disappeared onto the porch.

"Darling, I am going now, the car's here," said Tony.

He wore a pair of flannels and a cricket shirt, with the neck open and the collar turned down over a blue jacket. Margaret noticed how a shaft of sunlight, streaming across his head, illuminated the golden hues in his fair, curly hair. He looked young and yet there was a certain firm set about his jaw that belied youth and gave a look of maturity and determination to his open face.

Margaret wanted to take hold of him and tell him she didn't want to be left here by herself, she wanted him to stay. She didn't like him going off with the American, whom she didn't trust. She wanted to say that she thought all the people in this house were fakes and weren't to be trusted at all.

But he would have asked her why – and because she was only going on her women's intuition – she chose to say instead, "Don't be too late, and don't fall over Beachy Head!"

He laughed, it sounded foolish, but those words might have been spoken in deadly seriousness, if the events that were to befall him were foreseen.

He held her close to him and kissed her for several seconds, then he was gone. She stood listening to his footsteps on the stairs, and as she did, she thought again of those awful minutes last night. The storm, with the wind lashing the rain against the windows, the lightning and its terrifying revelation, the crashing thunder... She stopped her train of thought.

She crossed over to the window again. Wilbur, in a suit of brown serge and plus fours, carried a hamper basket with their teas inside. She watched him put it into the back of the car. She saw his fingers twist the catch on the rumble seat. Such strong hands he had – unusual for such a stout man. Brown and hard they were, like pieces of steel covered with chamois leather.

Powerful and unyielding with a grip of iron. If they were to catch anyone round the throat... Helpless... Tony...

She pretended to laugh to herself but she gave a shiver and shook her head, making her hair fly out like a skirt, as though to shake the thought out of her mind. She watched Wilbur and the mechanic speak together and then the man from the garage mounted his bicycle and rode off.

Wilbur reentered the house. The car stood there looking rather worn out and desolate to Margaret. The sun streamed down on the scene but the air was still sweet and fresh from the downpour last night. Everything in that part of the garden, below her window, was very quiet and peaceful. The thick yew hedge, skirting the inner side of the great wall surrounding the grounds, was backing the row of tall Hollyhocks away to the right of her. The water in the little lilly pool, directly in front of the porch, was a simmering sheet of glittering glass. Innumerable hoards of tiny gnats and mosquitos hovered close to the surface.

Margaret noticed a vividly coloured dragonfly skimming the rose tinted waters. It hung in the air for a second, suspended on flickering wings and cast a minute shadow on the mirror of the pond. The still waters seemed to mock its loveliness for it swiftly slipped away with a farewell flutter. Were the waters fast flowing? Still and peaceful? Deep and murky? Clear and shallow? Who knows? Who will ever know, but only that it was gone.

All these things Margaret saw and took in, but in her mind a turmoil of uncertainties were raging as she waited for Tony and Wilbur to reappear. The gentle breeze caressed the leaves of the swaying trees, creating delicate ripples that danced across the surface of the pool. The gates of the drive to the right and left were obscured from her view by large and extensive clusters of Rhododendrons and Azaleas, backed by a variety of flowering shrubs and bushes. A fresh, sweet perfume seemed to rise in a mist around the house, bringing into the rooms an atmosphere of summer loveliness that under any other circumstances would have made Margaret very happy. But it all only seemed to mock her for having rampant, ungrounded worries in her mind here at *Wuthering Winds*.

She was watching the clump of pretty shrubs bordering the drive on the side nearest to the house – she could see them easily with the position of the small bay window. The air felt very close, so she decided to open the window to catch some of the soft, whispering breeze, but then she noticed the clump of bushes by the drive. They were curiously moving a lot more than any of the other shrubs. Was it the breeze? Then in spite of herself, she gave an involuntary gasp. She caught a glimpse of something pink! A face – between the bushes!

The greenery parted and a man stood there in the drive. He was dressed in a long, tan raincoat – *strange for such a hot day*, thought Margaret – and a wide brimmed, blue pork-pie hat. She noticed dark trousers protruding from the coat and a bright reflection on the toes of the patent leather shoes. His coat collar was turned up right around his neck and chin, and the hat was thrust downwards over his head so that Margaret could only see the edge of his jaw and his cheek from her perspective above.

He stood for a second, turning his head this way and that. It was evident that he didn't want to be seen. She wondered what she ought to do, but for some reason, she did nothing. Only watched him with an all devouring curiosity. She saw him move quickly over to the car directly beneath her window. She looked down onto the top of his hat and onto his shoulders.

Such broad shoulders, she thought – funny how she should notice these things – but there was something strangely familiar about those thick limbs. Fascinated with fright, she was unable to make any move against this peculiar stranger. That he should not be there, she was well aware. That he might possibly be the key to all the unusual and weird happenings in this old, secretive manor house, tucked far away beneath the straggling hills of haunted Sussex, seemed to her a definite likelihood. Yet she was held spellbound, watching, waiting, to see what he would do.

His movements were quick and decisive. He stretched out his hand – something familiar there – and clasped the knob on the back of the car. With a twist and a jerk, he had flung it open. Glancing over his shoulder, and hesitating only long enough to examine the catch, he placed one leg over the edge and then with a quick spring, he was inside the rumble seat. Margaret saw the cover pulled from the inside. Dimly, she caught a glimpse of the sinister, vaguely familiar figure, curled up inside the rear of the old car. She saw the back shut, drawn closed by the fingers of strong hands, fingers she knew and feared, fingers uncanny yet unearthly... Ah, that was it!

Suddenly, she was struck by the silence of the garden again. Just the soft breeze and peaceful quiet. Too ordinary and too lovely to contain a secret such as this! So still was the scene that Margaret searched her mind for evidence that she had really seen a figure clamber into the back of the car. Ridiculous! Impossible! She had seen nothing – her imagination! And yet she knew it was not so.

She had watched and she had seen with her own eyes. There was no denying it, if her eyes were to be believed. How long she stood there, she was unable to tell. It might have been hours, it might have been only a few seconds. She knew that she should hurry down to tell Tony what she had seen, or rather what she thought she had seen, for already doubts were forming themselves into compact groups in her mind.

Everything had happened so quickly that surely it had only been a phantom of her imagination? Yet that figure – disturbing and realistic – it *had* been real! She was about to turn and run downstairs when she saw Wilbur and Tony appear from the porch. She hesitated again. She saw them climb jovially and unsuspectingly into the old Ford. She watched them examine the interior by touching the gears and old fashioned dashboard.

Then she heard the rattle, almost felt the vibration, as Wilbur started the worn-out engine. The sudden shattering of the quiet, sunlit garden seemed to jerk Margaret back to reality. She must rush down and tell them that there was a man in the back of the car!

If only she could have seen his face, she felt sure that she would have recognised him. *Why was he hiding like this? Whoever he was, what was he doing here? Why should he stowaway in the old fawn-coloured car with Tony and Wilbur? He could not be up to any good, surely?* A rushing surge of blood flooded these questions into her mind. Only one thing remained: *Danger!*

She must warn him! Tony – *her* Tony! There was danger in the form of that sinister man who must be following him. *And Wilbur Mortimer? He was in on it too?* Yes, she had always suspected him of being something other than what he pretended to be.

Very clearly, she saw it all! *That little American was driving him away, taking him out on the lonely expanse of the Downs, on the same hills that she had climbed with Tony. Then between them, Wilbur and this strange man would overpower Tony and...*

The roar of the engine revving cut in upon her thoughts. She must hurry, quickly before it was too late!

She left the window and crossed the room. The long, shallow flight of stairs lay before her as a barrier to him. Her fleeting footsteps made only a light pattering noise as she raced downwards. Again, she was forcibly and momentarily struck by the thought of her experience last night when the noise of the revving engine burst rudely off the panelled walls of the house.

She ran down the hall, the ticking of the huge grandfather clock in the corner matched her stride. She yanked open the outer door which crashed against the wall behind it. The way to him was open, she would not let him go! She would take hold of that sinister figure who had caused so much upheaval in the house already, and now lay concealed and waiting for his chance, biding his time, and then....

She rushed through the porch and out onto the drive. The car jumped forward but her voice was drowned by the rattle of the spluttering engine.

"Tony, Tony! Stop, Tony!" She stood in the middle of the gravel drive calling after him but in her heart she knew it was hopeless.

She watched the old car with its three occupants disappear from view. If the back were glass she would be able to see that strangely, familiar figure curled up in the closed seat. Her fear tormented her – there was nothing she could do! She suddenly felt rather sick and horribly frightened. What would happen?

She tried to tell herself that this was all melodramatic rubbish and that in a moment she would wake up and find herself in her own bed at home in London. This sort of thing didn't happen to ordinary people like herself. The sound of the motor driving up the dusty road leading into those great grey-green hills, that merged into the blue sky, reminded her that these things *had* happened and *were* happening.

"Hello there! Have they gone?"

The voice at her side made Margaret turn quickly. Roma Beaumont stood there, a dark shadow – slim and striking – in a garden of green and gold, sunkissed foliage. Her voice was pleasant and temporarily reassuring.

At least, Margaret thought, *now I know that Roma is only who she professes to be.*

But the next second, she felt her former fears return in force about this dark and sleek woman. It was not so much the words as the tone of voice, soft and deeply soothing on the surface, but tinged with a hidden menace. Almost a threat to Margaret in her overwrought state of nerves.

"Now they've gone, we will be by ourselves for the afternoon." A gleam of something dark flickered behind Roma's smile. "Come let's go into the house, we can have tea in the library."

12

Stately Sussex

Overpowering in their mighty, unending chain of green clad peaks, the great Sussex Downs stretch in majestic pompousness through the extreme Western boundaries of the county of Sussex. Overlooking the famous seaside resorts of Chichester, Bognor Regis, Littlehampton, Worthing, Shoreham, Brighton and Newhaven, they end in the terrifying sheer drop of five hundred and seventy-five feet. The loftiest headland in the South of England – Beachy Head.

This marks the end of the West Downs and here commences the rolling slopes of the Eastern Hills. These overlook, with lofty superiority, Eastbourne, the historic Pevensey Bay, Bexhill and Hastings. The neat harbour of Rye marks the start of the Romney Marsh where the chalk slopes pass into Kent, until they resign their dominion at the town of Dover. And so it is that Sussex is sheltered from the elements and cut off from the land across the water, which is France. Small wonder that a newcomer to these parts is a stranger for many years!

From the summit of a peak overlooking a quaint village, Tony and Wilbur now stood surveying the delightful scene bathed in the warm, afternoon sunshine. They had parked the car in a narrow street on the outskirts of the village and had clambered up the hills to see the view that is possibly unequalled in all England, but surely matching the unrivalled beauty of rugged Devon or wild Wales. Further along the rolling green hills they could see the two famous windmills, nicknamed by the locals, *Jack and Jill.*

There is something inviting and pleasantly sleepy about Sussex, thought Anthony and he allowed his mind to wander unheeded while he drank in the peaceful beauty of the vast expanse of patchwork landscape. All thoughts of the terrors of *Wuthering Winds* were completely banished from his mind. He was oblivious to the presence of Wilbur Mortimer by his side, who was also struck by the breath-taking loveliness of this part of rural England.

After a while they descended and returned to the village. Tony was taken aback by the ease with which his stout companion carried his weight up and down the slopes, for he had found the going quite hard, and it was surprising to him to note the agility with which the American manoeuvred the numerous obstacles. *Strange! That a man of such dimensions and proportions should be able and willing to undergo such active exercise,* pondered Tony.

They had only come about five miles and by following along the base, in the shadow of the Downs on a narrow country lane, they eventually reached Fulking. They stopped again and examined the old fountain that pours its icy waters directly from the hills onto the road just as it has done from time immeasurable to the present day. They entered the modest inn, *The Fox and Hounds,* and sat overshadowed by the steep hills. The old Roman road, which stretches from the bottom to the top of the slopes, runs along the highest peaks on to Canterbury. This was also a favourite route of the Canterbury Pilgrims, and it is easy to see how they must have been inspired by the dominating view offered from the road.

Being only about six miles from Brighton, Tony and Wilbur discussed whether to go into the town but they finally decided to cut through Pyecombe to Clayton and Ditchling. This village is famous for the mighty Ditchling Beacon which nestles beneath the hills, sheltering its charming buildings of historical interest such as the old church and Catherine of Aragon's house, presented to her by Henry the Eighth.

From here they proceeded directly to Lewes, and spent some time investigating this most interesting historical town of all Sussex. The grey stone castle towered atop the steep hill, its imposing presence rivalling the cold, forbidding walls of the modern prison that sprawled along the gentle slope at the town's edge.

Jane Seymour, another wife of Wolf Hall, had a house here and as a museum, it offered a point of particular interest to Wilbur who declared, "Sure am enchanted with good, old England's historical joints!"

They completed the last seventeen miles directly into Eastbourne without a break while the sun hung like a glowing ball of fire over the purple-grey sea. They finally stood with spellbound delight, staring out across the sea that lashed itself into a frenzy of frustrated fury at their feet far below. Rising a sheer five hundred and seventy five feet, like a white pillar of power and inspiration, they stood revelling in the majestic beauty of the mighty Beachy Head.

13
Cliffs of Fate

"**D**on't get too near the edge, the ground might crumble underfoot," warned Tony.

Wilbur stood about ten yards from the start of the white walls that dropped far below to the sea. The wind bent its soft sighing to thundering breakers as they threw their spray high up the chalk cliff and then trickled off the numerous ledges and crevices that pitted the softened face.

"Small wonder that this is England's number one suicidal spot," remarked Tony reflectively. "I believe that it's a wonderful sight to peer over the edge at the sea below, especially if the tide is up."

"Well, buddy!" said the American grinning, "if we lay flat and crawl forward, I guess we ought to get a pretty good view."

Together, they wriggled up to the edge. The fresh breeze cut across the Channel, playing a strong sea-scented rush of clean air directly into their faces as they gazed down in awestruck silence at the terrible and yet lovely scene of wild splendour below them.

After a while, the American broke their quiet enchantment. "What d'ya make of the events last night, champ? I've been mulling over it, and I can't quite put my finger on the facts. By the end of the ordeal, your aunt was in a terrible state, poor woman."

"And Margaret," shuddered Tony, with his eyes on the horizon and his hands squeezing handfuls of soft grass, "she was overcome with fright. She's not one for flighty fancies." The crash of the furious waves below filled the air around the two men as they contemplated this statement.

"There has to be an explanation," declared Wilbur, rolling onto his elbow and facing Tony. "Something about each of the individuals at *Wuthering Winds* has been slightly odd to me. Could there be a plot underway?"

"To what end?" replied Tony. The idea had entered his mind several times. "Well, I hardly know what to think. I have never had much to do with such things."

Wilbur's voice was very low and he sounded unusually serious. "I have," he said after a brief moment.

"Does this business strike you as having any connection with the – er – *supernatural*?" Tony was at a loss for a better word.

"In some ways it does and in other ways it doesn't. I should give a mighty lot to know just what Mrs Lucile Guyate really saw last night."

"Then you believe she genuinely did see something?" enquired Tony. He felt frustrated when the answer to the very pointed question was returned to him. *Wilbur*, he thought, *is definitely not committing himself.*

"I wouldn't like to say, I don't know her well enough."

The American allowed his gaze to wander along the purple horizon before taking out a cigarette and offering Tony one. He struck a match and drew vigorously, allowing the smoke to issue from his mouth and nostrils in a lazy blue coil. He turned his body slightly so that he could look straight at Tony.

"There's the housemaid, Jenny Walker. She's dead now, poor kid. Why?"

For just a second, Tony did not comprehend the question. When he did, a sudden hot realisation burst upon him like a flood of pressure. Something in that name had struck a memory within him. Something that the foreboding events of the last twenty-four hours had made him completely forget.

With a quick movement he passed his hand to his trouser pocket. The note! The note the girl had handed him in the doorway of the dining room that fateful night, only so short a while ago. He faltered, his hand almost touching his pocket. Should he turn out the contents there and then in front of the quirky man or should he wait for a more opportune moment?

He glanced up and saw that Wilbur was still regarding him with interest. A glint in the other's eye told him that it was useless to try and hide anything from his companion. He fumbled among the varied contents of his pocket, his hand touching a tiny folded slip of paper. As his fingers closed over it he thrilled at the thought that here, perhaps was something material, something solid, on which to base his line of rather abstract observations. Here perhaps was something that might have changed the course of all these startling and mysterious events that had chained themselves to such a tragic conclusion. If perhaps he could, with the aid of the scrap of paper, have prevented the unfortunate girl's death...

Very slowly, he withdrew his clenched hand. Wilbur had not moved nor deterred his gaze. Slowly, he unfurled the note and smoothed its crumpled surface upon the scanty, bluey-coloured grass.

The words were written in a childish round hand with the letters badly formed, and although the creases had made some parts a little faint, the note as a whole was perfectly legible. It ran as follows:

Dear Mr Marshton, I must speak to you privately, ALONE, tonight. Would you meet me in the garden by the south French windows? I have something very important to tell you.

For some seconds the two men lay staring at the astounding message. Only the high-pitched calls of the ever-circling seagulls broke the silence of the desolate spot.

"Rum," Wilbur still did not move. "Very rum," he repeated softly.

Tony's brow was puckered in a frown. "I don't understand what she would want and what she was caught up in."

"Perhaps she knew something? Perhaps she was in trouble or danger? Perhaps she even knew that she might meet with some fatal injury. What would she do?" The American was speaking very quietly.

Tony could hardly catch what he said. He spoke the words like a chain of thoughts filtering down and were then caught up and washed away with the sighing swells.

"She would tell someone, explain what was worrying her, try and find somebody who might understand, sympathise and help her," continued Wilbur.

"Do you really think she was psychic and had some idea of what might happen?" Tony's voice was almost but not quite incredulous!

"Possibly." Wilbur inclined his head slowly and reaching forward picked up the slip of paper. He folded it and just as though he had every right, placed it in the interior pocket of his jacket.

"Now what do you think of Skeels the butler?" prodded Wilbur.

Tony did not answer immediately. He was not going to sum up the character so quickly, and as he now realised, so inaccurately, as he had before.

Eventually, he said thoughtfully, "A strange man. Quite unique. But I am convinced he would do nothing to harm my aunt or anyone she has an interest in, myself for example."

"Quite, that is my opinion too," replied the short, tubby man who had, it appeared, remarkable thinking properties. "But what about those people or things outside the circle of your aunt's interests, or even those who were alien to her principles? Do you think he would be or is so placid towards them? I think we have had sufficient evidence to answer that question, haven't we?" he went on dryly. "I was exceedingly surprised to note the distinct change in him directly after the curious affair at the dinner table last night."

"Was that only last night?" repeated Tony. "It seems weeks ago; so much has taken place since then, I have lost all track of time."

For some seconds there was silence between the two, each man weighing up the character of the butler. Then Wilbur, as though summing up judgement on the strange personality of their observations said, "Under the circumstances I like Skeels but I cannot help admitting that he has such a peculiar makeup. I have several points I would like explained." He paused. "For instance, I believe he has made a pretty thorough check of our belongings in our rooms."

Tony was immediately intrigued by the similarity to his own observations of this statement. "I noticed that my room appeared to have been searched and Margaret also told me she suspected the same. But of course, we had no idea who it could be." He laughed. "To tell you the truth I had a crazy notion that it might have been you!"

Wilbur smiled rather grimly. "I met him just coming out of my room on Friday evening. It occurred to me that it was queer, but he said something about hoping I was comfortable and making sure that I had every convenience, so of course, I let it go at that. Later I found, without a doubt, that my room had been searched."

Neither of the two men spoke. Each of them realised that now the only people they had not discussed were the guests themselves. Tony watched as a great ship moved slowly across the horizon, its top deck just visible, with smoke belching from its funnels through the blue haze that hung like an obscuring curtain over the vast expanse before him.

"I don't think we need to say much about Margaret." The American glanced sideways at Anthony with a twinkle in his eyes. "She didn't know Mrs Guyate before she came down here did she?"

"No."

"She's a nice kid," he went on, "I admire your choice."

Tony knew it was moments like this when he most disliked the gentleman beside him. Yet he also knew that here was a man of great human understanding. He wished he could penetrate the strange cloak of hidden personality that made him such an interesting companion.

"What about Roma Beaumont?" wondered Tony.

"This sort of person sure can get one mighty mixed up, she's the strangest individual in the whole house." Wilbur looked down over the edge of the terrible drop that fell sheer to the tumultuous waters below.

"Do you believe in her spiritualist doctrine?" Tony made great emphasis on this point.

"Not entirely."

"But you do think there's something in it?"

The American shrugged his shoulders. "What else can one think? Things happen that can't be explained, only a fool would deny that."

Tony considered this silently. Undoubtedly, there was a sort of sneaking sympathy with this woman on the part of his companion. He decided he had better change the character under discussion. It was pointless to mention his old aunt. He racked his brain. The realisation came suddenly, there was only Wilbur and himself left.

He took the plunge quickly, "You know all about me, but none of us know about you." He stopped as sharply as he started and turned his head to look directly into Wilbur's steely grey eyes. He saw with surprise and almost alarm, just how hard those eyes really were. But the American was smiling genially.

"Except that I came from Salt Lake City four years ago to join this illustrious insurance company, giving folks an opportunity to invest in the company's benefits. There ain't much more to tell."

"Oh," said Tony quietly. *Why should anyone come right over to England just to be an insurance agent when there were far greater openings for a man in the States?*

He saw that the sun was hanging low over the waters away to the West and a shimmering trail of golden light made a pathway on the purple-blue sea.

"It's getting late. There's a long drive home and we had better be pushing off. Are you going to see if that pub's open, I'm as dry as hell."

The American nodded and moved backwards from the cliff's edge. "Shan't be a second," he said lightly, "give you a yell if it's open."

Tony did not watch him go. He lay there without moving, watching the circling gulls that echoed each other's wild, desolate cries. The ship out on the horizon had drawn level with him. Away to his right the shining semi-circle of light marked the historic Pevensey Bay. Near to the jutting curve of Beachy Head, on which he lay, straggled the tree dotted town of Eastbourne. The stiff, ruffling breeze played a continual draft upon his bared head and sun kissed face. *Wuthering Winds*, house of mystery and terror, seemed to count for nothing as he closed his eyes and drank in the pure, clean sweep of sea salt air.

A gentle feeling of lazy satisfaction stole over him. Peace! If Wilbur called, he would not move. Strange people, weird shapes, dead faces and writhing figures rose up before his mind and were swept clear by the indescribable joy of being alone. At this altitude, he felt himself soaring! Soaring in life and love. Unconsciously he found himself repeating those lovely, infinitely beautiful words: "*And the peace of God which passeth all understanding keep–*"

He felt a cold hand grip his warm throat. Suddenly, pressure from a heavy body was upon his back. The desire for air, that a moment before, he had been breathing with healthy pleasure, now ballooned in his chest. He wanted air! Stagnant, stale, anything with which to fill his lungs!

He caught the touch of warm breath upon the nape of his neck, just above the vice like hands. He struggled desperately. He felt his head being forced slowly over the edge of the terrible chasm below. His whole body was being pushed outwards!

He felt his eyes bulging from their tortured sockets. He had a dreadful pounding of many drums in his ears and his unseeing gaze met a blank wall of darkness. His frenzied, feverish grasp made wild clutches at the tufts of feeble grass. One hand stove upwards, touching something soft and unrecognisable. He pulled!

His last thoughts – *Wilbur!* He knew it all along! He had said too much. He knew too much. He was being silenced. Forever.

The relentless crash of the thundering waves hurled themselves against the solid, white walls, wafting up the sound of a choked gurgle, "Beachy Head, cliff of the damned..."

14

Ascending the Stairs of Suspense

The warm sun cast its life-giving rays through the closely hung leaves of the great oak, standing in all its splendid garb of fine, summer greenery by the edge of the mossy stretch of lawn.

Margaret found her hammock chair was comfortable and placed so that she was not entirely in the deep shade and yet not completely exposed to the full glare of the sun. She felt drowsy, and only the vague disquieting thought in her mind spoiled her peace with the world.

Sherriff's, *A Fortnight in September*, lay open across her knees. Just the merest suggestion of a caressing, warm breeze fluttered the hem of her dainty frock. A flicker of a smile played upon her lips, her eyes were closed with placid satisfaction in the quiet and beauti-ful surroundings. A soft rustling among the mass of full foliage overhead betrayed the presence of the darting birds chasing each other with delight while revelling in the greatness of nature's basking beauty.

Margaret allowed her thoughts to wander over the rising, green hills that stood before her in a magnificent array. Hand in hand, she imagined herself wandering with her handsome love along the dormant slopes. A shadow falling across her closed eyes made her glance up quickly, as though resenting the intrusion into her intimate thoughts.

Roma Beaumont's voice sounded subdued but friendly. "Isn't it glorious out there?" She seated herself in the chair by Margaret's side. "I hope I didn't wake you? I have just been up to see Mrs Guyate."

Margaret's veil of selfish thoughts dropped like a curtain wrenched suddenly aside. "How is she? Better? What did she say?" Margaret returned with a rush.

"I think she seems much recovered; she is sitting up but is still in a very weak state. I purposely refrained from asking her anything that might overtax her brain and spoke only of trivial subjects."

Margaret thought Roma sounded rather pleasant and immediately it sprang to her mind that she and Tony had misjudged this tall, handsome woman. She decided to try to be much more friendly with her fellow guest at *Wuthering Winds*.

"I wonder where the men could be now?" Margaret mused out loud. "I expect they will be starting back soon. By the way, what's the time? I have no idea how long I have been sitting here, I probably dozed off for a while."

"It's twenty past four. I asked Skeels to bring us tea out here." Roma flashed Margaret a bewitching smile.

When the willowy woman had first come out, Margaret had felt a trifle nervous, or perhaps even a little afraid, but now she felt her confidence rising. The other woman seemed so companionable.

"Do you know if anyone came up from the village to help Mrs Berkley? I haven't seen anybody about?" enquired Margaret.

"I believe a girl has arrived, but I think Mrs Berkley had great difficulty in persuading any of the local people to come." She paused and regarded her neatly clasped hands in her lap with thoughtful attention. "This place hasn't got a very good reputation with the general population of the district. I don't know why," she ended, unconvincingly.

It was, Margaret felt, as though a shadow had suddenly been thrown upon them. This was what she had unknowingly been trying to avoid. Her former uncomfortable nervousness once more returned with renewed gusto. She didn't answer. The chink of china relieved the silence and the appearance of Skeels with a laden tray killed the unwelcome topic.

During tea they chatted in an ordinary manner but there seemed to be a kind of guarded ease in their communication. It was as though a thundercloud hung over them, threatening to break and shower all the wrath of the heavens onto their heads.

Margaret felt slightly unnerved and she dreaded the repetition of the former terrifying events coming up in conversation. Her imagination took on nightmare proportions while she tried to continue the pleasantries.

Eventually they finished tea. A slight breeze had begun to blow and Roma proposed re-entering the old house. Margaret would much rather have stayed outside in the garden but Roma gave her little opportunity to reject the suggestion. They began the walk up to the house. Going in through a side door, which opened into the end of the hall, there was a small cloakroom that led to the main passage.

Margaret noticed that there was dry and hard mud on the floor, evidently bought in hours ago. Vaguely, she remembered something about mud on Wilbur Mortimer's shoes last night. With vivid clarity, this thought brought to her the strange and unexplained happenings that had turned the whole place into a house of death and dread.

They passed along the wide hall to the great oak stairs. The loud ticking and swinging pendulum of the huge, old clock in the corner lent the place an air of mystery. It seemed to announce the threat of swiftly passing time, resulting in a violent and sudden end.

In here, Margaret thought the very air seemed stale and stagnant. The presence of her companion caused her uneasiness and malignant thoughts, only half formed, to catch in her mind and entwine her in an undercurrent of uncertainty. The thud of their footfalls seemed to jar the old place into a menacing, pregnant hate that hung in the air. Every corner and doorway hid a ghastly figure of immortal horror. Strange, twisted, broken thoughts were drugging her brain with unfounded fear and the ring of Roma's low, clear voice sent an unaccountable terror into her heart.

"I'm just going upstairs to get my crochet work. Go into the library, dear, I shan't be a minute, then we'll have a nice, quiet chat together."

Tingling sensations trilled up and down Margaret's spine. She felt her knees were weak as she turned with a timid smile to Roma. She watched the woman's lithe and graceful body move with perfect poise up the great broad staircase. The sombre, grey coloured frock Roma was wearing made her appear like an unreal, ominous figure, such as Margaret might have been haunted by in her childhood nightmares.

She stood there in the great bare hall that always seemed to be dark and dismal, looking up to the point where Roma had turned at the massive curved bannister post at the first landing. One of the old vases, with the strange Chinese figures upon it, was just within her view. She remembered dully and without interest how she had noticed these voluminous pieces of clay when she had first climbed to the landing along which her room was situated. She tried to reckon how big they were. *Five foot high at least?* She was afraid – yes – definitely afraid to move. *Three feet wide in the centre* – it came to her in a flash – *big enough to conceal a man!*

Her heart was pounding in her breast as she took an involuntary step backwards. The tap, as her heel hit the polished oak boards, sounded like a pistol shot in the silence. Her eyes were fixed upon the object of her sudden unintentional interest. She felt a sickening, intangible desire to go up to that narrow landing and peer into the depths of the piece of clay craft, moulded so cleverly, so long ago, by some ancient Chinese man, who had been so miraculously bestowed with the gift of his art.

Almost without knowing what she was doing, her feet were on the first wide stair board. Very slowly, she started her ascent. Step by step, her pulse raced. Her slim body strained to bursting point with the exertions of the nerve-racking events that seemed to be tumbling over each other in an endeavour to get themselves enacted.

On the third stair she stopped and stood motionless. No sound came from the upper region of the great house, where Margaret had last seen Roma Beaumont. In the hall below, the dull thudding of the massive oak clock continued, swinging its heavy pendulum in slow rotation, causing that uncanny, monotonous sound, like the pulse of this whole strange, old manor.

As she slowly climbed, higher and higher, the air seemed to become more and more stagnant, but there was also a faint taint of something sweet and sickly. With each step she took up the great staircase, she noticed that the air grew more stale. Not unpleasant or revolting, but as if fine, old scents or spices had been shut up in the place for many years. However, she realised that all her senses and emotions were presently increased and exaggerated.

Over halfway up to the first landing, a board creaked under her light footstep. She froze, a cold, hard band of trepidation forming round her racing heart. *Why should she stop? Why should she be silent in this giant empty place? Why did she have that horrible, unprovoked intuition of something fearful near at hand?*

With a sudden spark of resolute courage, she made a quick dart up the remaining stairs with still no sound from any part of the great house.

She stood on the landing breathing hard. Up here the air was very sweet and very strong with its pungent scent that seemed to be swirling in twisty clouds all about her. There was something magnetic and yet repulsive – something overripe and cloying. She could find no solution to this strange effect in the sun-dusty, still air.

The edge of the tall jar was coincidently on level with her bare neck. A half pace forward and sideways, she peered over the brink of the rim…

The moment her eyes fell upon the dreadful, unforgettable horror, her panic-stricken mind was preserved by a consuming numbness that spread like a gentle yet ominous shield over her ghastly thoughts.

Her first startling recollection returned to her suddenly. The thought of those eyes – those dead staring eyes. That dreadful parchment-like skin with the high protruding cheek bones and little pointed beard – this face was before her very eyes!

Crammed down into the interior depths of the old piece of Chinese pottery was the embalmed body of Doctor Herbert Guyate!

With the head forced back, so that the face was upturned, the fearful figure was hunched up in a terrible position.

Frozen to immobility, she was held spellbound by the revulsion of her awful discovery. Still the unperturbed, old clock below continued its rhythm. This terrible, magical moment seemed like an age. The thought of all these gruesome happenings and the evident tangled skein of plots rose before her like an apparition as startling yet realistic as the grisly object in its unexpected container.

Just how long she stood there, she was unable to tell. The next clear thought in her mind was the sudden low ring of a quiet voice. She spun round in a paradox of fear.

"My dear, what an unfortunate discovery for you to make," Roma stood just behind her. The note of mockery was only too evident and the tone of threat stood clearly in Margaret's thoughts. Unable to answer, she stood still, facing the other woman. She saw Roma's face twist with a horrible snarl.

"My dear," she purred tauntingly, "what a pity you had to find this." Her head was thrust forward indicatively.

Roma's eyes glowed with hate, yet Margaret was certain that she could see a flicker of delight. Cat and mouse was a feature showing its appeal to the terrible, plainly sadistic, black-haired medium. Her step forward was silent and grimly suggestive.

The cold, hard rim of the vase at the nape of her neck told Margaret she had unknowingly moved backwards. Wild thoughts entered the channels of her mind like a scalding flood. The thoughts of her own danger were almost overcome by the complete realisation of the meaning of all the unexplained events that had enveloped her during the last few days and nights. Motive was as yet not apparent but the objective of this moment was naked in truth before her frightened mind.

Roma reached out her hand as Margaret flattened herself against the high piece of pottery. She felt the cold perspiration on her forehead run in a thin trickle down the side of her face. She saw the tight muscles on the arm of the evil woman before her and the horrible glint of wicked menace in her flashing black eyes.

The claw-like hand met the curve of her soft neck, the tapering fingernails poiscd to jab like a weapon. Margaret felt the nearness of her end and the murmur of a prayer was on her lips.

"Take your filthy hands off that girl, you swine!" came a growl from behind.

Margaret's head whirled round and her surprise surpassed all her other emotions. With a small, but vicious looking pistol in his right hand, and a look of indiscernible hatred on his face, stood Skeels, immaculate butler of *Wuthering Winds*!

15

Counterpart

Beachy Head jutted its stern profile into the relentless rolling waters that beat with incessant pounding at the feet of the great chalky cliffs. Screeching seagulls wheeled in ever widening circles, staring with their tiny bright eyes at the intruders in their wild domain. For there, on the edge of the terrible white wall, were two figures locked in deadly combat.

Tony felt his body slipping further and further out into space. The dreadful grip on his throat did not slacken for an instant. Powerless to see who his silent assailant was, he realised that the creature who now held him in a death grip had something to fear from him and was ensuring his deadly silence forever.

Wilbur Mortimer was surely that person. He was paying the price of his safety with the life of his fellow guest at the old Sussex house. Tony had come out here with the American in an endeavour to find between them a normal and feasible explanation to the strange occurrences at his aunt's old house. His last clear and really vivid thoughts were of Margaret. He had come to a final conclusion at last, but now it was too late. His last recollection was a desperate hope that Margaret might be forewarned of her peril and escape. A bell started a monotonous toll, ringing a pounding thud upon his bursting eardrums. Then it suddenly ceased!

***

"Well! Well! I'm sure I don't know what to say! All these strange goings on." The good *lady of the house* on top of Beachy Head stood gazing at the figure of the young man who lay upon the couch in her back parlour. Her cheeks were rosy with excitement at her unusual guests, one of whom seemed to be hurt in some way, but this fact in itself was only a repeat of her many former experiences.

So often people were brought into her establishment to wait for the police, but as a rule, they were nearly always devoid of all life. Then for days she would be besieged with inspectors from the Eastbourne Constabulary and reporters from many different newspapers. When she first came here it had been rather tiresome, but now she was getting used to it. For four years, she had catered to a wide variety of visitors seeking drinks and snacks. Her staff was small but diligent, working hard with the characteristic honesty of Sussex folk. During the busy summer months, their efforts had yielded some quite handsome returns.

Wilbur was bending over the still figure, examining the bright red marks on his throat. Finally, he turned and faced the pink-faced woman. He smiled disarmingly and said, "He'll pull round in a minute. Just an accident, you know, I expect you have quite a lot up here on this peak, don't you?"

The woman nodded in affirmation and retired to prepare refreshment for her visitors. *At least,* she thought, *if he is going to recover, he might prove a profitable customer.* She judged by the clothes and general bearing of the two men that they were above the usual plebeian, cosmopolitan type of trippers whom she was accustomed to having at her conveniently situated hotel.

When Wilbur was alone, he moved quickly over to Anthony and stood gazing down at the young man's clear cut features. He noticed the flicker of his eye and in less than a minute, Tony was fully recovered mentally, but he was to have an exceedingly stiff neck for some time to come.

He lay for several minutes gazing up at Wilbur with a puzzled frown on his face. When he spoke his voice was husky and strained, his single word was filled with incredulous surprise coupled with a taint of horror and amazement.

"You?!"

Wilbur smiled grimly but remained silent. He pulled a chair up to the couch, his expression kind and friendly.

"Now just lie quietly for a bit, Anthony, I think we have got a lot of explaining to do, so I'll try and tell you everything – as far as I know."

Tony was immediately struck by the distinct change in the other man's demeanour. The American accent and easy, drawling tone were gone. He seemed to have taken on the quiet calmness of an English gentleman. His next words were even more astounding.

"I know what you're thinking," he went on, "you're wondering where my American character has got to." Tony nodded in mute surprise. "Well, it's just that I haven' got an American character anymore."

"You mean you were putting that on?" Tony found his voice and lost it again.

Wilbur's grin increased, he slipped a deft hand into an inner pocket and withdrew an official looking document which he flashed before Anthony.

"I'm afraid I have an admission to make," he began. "You see, I am not what I led you to believe, I am in reality a detective from Scotland Yard, London. Don't think badly of me, I had my job to do and it had to be done."

Tony gasped with surprise, he found it hard to believe that he had been so easily hoodwinked. "Then why did you attack me on the cliffs a little while ago?"

At this, his companion looked interested and he once more took on a manner of acute alertness. "That," he replied, "is something I must speak with you about immediately. It is imperative that we act quickly. This is roughly what happened as far as I can gather. Someone must have followed us here and watched us continually since we left *Wuthering Winds*. I can't think by what means, but let it for now suffice that he did. Presuming this, he waited until we parted and then when I came here, he seized his opportunity and took advantage of his element of surprise over you. The perfect, natural position for an *accident.* I am convinced he would have pushed you off the edge of the cliff." The man Tony knew only as Wilbur Mortimer ended abruptly.

"What happened then?" urged Tony in an awed, husky whisper. He was gradually beginning to realise just what he owed his companion.

"When I started to come back for you, I was amazed to see this figure clutching you at the throat and forcing you nearer the brink of that dreadful drop. I started to run, shouting as I went. At first, he didn't hear me, I was some way off and I was frantic in case I should be a witness to your death and yet be unable to prevent it. I think a vision of Margaret before me lent me speed to my legs. I ran like the wind, my feet hardly seemed to touch the ground. My lungs were bursting with my desperate shouts.

Suddenly he must have heard me as I saw him turn. Even at that distance I could not fail to recognise him. There was blood on his face – dripping from his chin. He let go of you with a violent fling. For one terrible moment I thought you would topple over the edge of the cliff but miraculously you remained suspended, balanced with part of your body dangling over the jagged rocks and lashing waves! I saw him pelting towards the car and fling himself in. The last I saw was his head low to the wheel and the old motor going flat out down that bumpy road over the Downs heading back to Arundel."

The stout man stood in the middle of the floor awaiting Tony's expected outburst, but Anthony only sat with a puzzled look on his face. It had come as a great shock to him to think that he had suspected, had convinced himself, that this gentleman who had so keenly felt for him, was a vile murderer of the highest degree.

Slowly Wilbur put his hand to his inside pocket and withdrew a large leather wallet. He took out an oblong envelope and shook the contents into his hand. Tony saw a small clump of iron grey hairs, obviously wrenched from the flesh by the roots, and adhered together by clots of congealed blood. Tony stared in dismay at the grisly relic. At first he failed to connect it with the fearful experience that he had just undergone, then it suddenly dawned on him just what this piece of disturbing matter was.

"Recognise it?" inquired the American impersonator. Tony nodded mutely. "I found it in your clenched hand."

"I remember! "Tony flashed. "I caught hold of it during my struggle with my potential assassinator."

"But do you know to whom it belongs?" Wilbur's face was a hard mask, his chiselled features immovable.

Tony stood up carefully and took an unsteady step nearer him. He gazed intently at the revolting and repugnant wisps of hair and allowed his mind to think back to when he had last seen a likeness to the living flesh. His companion watched him in silence and then saw him go an ashen-grey colour as the full realisation came to him.

Never before had Tony seen hair like this on a living creature, yet it struck a familiar cord in his memory. The thought shifted the entire problem toward what he had most dreaded – something beyond explanation. Such strange and unorthodox ideas flooded his reeling imagination that he could only look at the other man in dismay. Their eyes met, filled with unspoken understanding and a shared, creeping dread. The implications were unimaginable – something unnatural was at play, something that defied both reason and the laws of nature. They had been taught to believe that death was the end, a final and absolute stillness. Yet here they were, facing a reality that seemed to mock that certainty, suggesting instead a continuation and a violation of that sacred boundary.

"My name is James Stirling, Inspector of Scotland Yard. This case is different to me than any of my others," he said. "It is as though I have some deep personal interest in you." The two men finally looked at each other, clear and unburdened, for neither had a secret left to hide. It was as if an unspoken pact had formed between them.

The gnawing feeling in Anthony's mind was relieved a little to know that he had such an ally as this good-hearted man whose vocation was prevention of crime.

"We must move fast now," James Stirling said, "We must get back to *Wuthering Winds* with all haste. With luck and with God's permission, we will be in time to frustrate the evil intentions of our adversary. There is something at the back of all this terror that we can tackle, the supernatural can't have its hair pulled out!"

Tony laughed grimly but the break in his tone showed the fear in his heart. Fear not for himself, but rather a fear that had been germinating since the first mention of the people back at *Wuthering Winds*.

An inspiration took his fancy and he said excitedly, "Here's an idea of how we can get back quickly! We can phone Eastbourne from here and get a car to meet us at the west crossing. If we cut down over the hills, we can save going into town."

With his spirits heightened by his suggestion, Tony was anxious to start the final chapter of this immemorial experience.

James' plump face turned in a smile of pleasure as he realised the philosophy of the suggestion. His prompt agreement was met with approval by Tony, eager as he was to start back and be near the girl who was now constantly in his thoughts.

Just a scarlet glow in the western sky betrayed the presence of the sinking sun as the two men trudged in silence down the short, stunted grass slopes to the road, like a white ribbon that snaked in the shadow of the hills.

Tony's mind was a maze of half formed thoughts. The end of this ordeal was near but just what the end would be was still undecided. Everything depended on whether he could get back to *Wuthering Winds* quickly enough to prevent further incidents, possibly even pertaining to life and death. He glanced sideways at his companion's face; James Stirling seemed to have taken on a new vital and urgent determination.

They reached the road without having spoken more than a dozen words. They had not long to wait, almost immediately the hum of a powerfully-engined car became steadily clearer to them. Round the curve of the deserted road, a large, low saloon came swiftly into view.

The driver, a short man with a bland expression and a small, clipped toothbrush moustache, drew the car up beside them and inquired whether they were the two gentlemen he had been told to meet at this point of the road. Tony and James informed him they were his fares and Anthony took the seat next to the driver to direct him as to the route.

James sat in the back and taking a notebook from his pocket, he appeared to lose interest in everything except the scribbled writing that covered the pages. He remained in deep thought for the whole of the journey in the swift, black car that sped through the peaceful evening of the lovely Sussex landscape.

16
Crimson Clues

Poets and writers have praised the peace of dusk. That soft, grey hour of gentle twilight that favours the countryside or quiet village, resting on the laurels of its days' work on the earth. Even the air seemed to hold a reverence at eventide, a breathless hush over the green fields and wooded slopes. The promise for the new day that will be born as dawn overtakes the darkness on the morrow, a certainty often taken for granted, yet always expected to arrive. So it was that Sussex was experiencing the quiet thrill of these moments with the sky turning a salmon shade and streaked with the golden glints spun by rays of the setting sun.

The eastern side of the old manor house was deep in a cool shadow that spread outward from the rough walls onto the lawn. Silence was the most noticeable factor in the whole vicinity of *Wuthering Winds;* even the birds appeared to have gone to roost early in the quiet confines of the spinney. The warm but refreshing breeze moved the foliage of the trees and shrubs in unison.

Inside the great building, everywhere was deathly still and quiet. Margaret sat without moving, bolt up-right on a tall, carved chair in the second-floor room, which was Mrs Guyate's bedroom. She was keyed now to a pitch of great jittery nervousness. She felt the anticipation building, reaching a crescendo that would finally unravel the mystery and fright that had haunted her since she first arrived at *Wuthering Winds*.

Her whole body was exhausted and she would like to have slept but she was unable to close her eyes for any length of time. She kept stealing a swift, anxious glance towards the great oak door, then she would return her gaze back to the still figure of the little old lady in the four-poster bed.

The gloom was closing rather swiftly with only the polished wall panelling to reflect the receding light. Margaret had been sitting here since those dreadful moments when Skeels had appeared on the stairs with his pistol. A spot on her neck tingled. She shuddered as she thought of that evil woman reaching out and touching her. The kindly old butler, as dominating as he looked, had shown great strength of character during those minutes. With evident pleasure, he had ordered Roma Beaumont, the spiritual medium, along the passage and into the library. He had first ensured the fastenings on the French doors, locked the door and removed the key.

Initially, the tall woman had looked furious but then rather fearful. Margaret thought there was an unusual glint in Skeels' eyes that warned her against the cat-like spring of her body, that seemed to so fit her character. Just in case she felt tempted to hurl herself upon the gallant old butler in a fit of rage.

Now Margaret sat waiting with her heart beating away the seconds, hoping that Tony would not be long. She dared not allow herself to think of that strange figure she had seen clamber into the back of the car. She had tried to dismiss it from her mind by thinking he knew, or that it was only a tramp stealing a lift. With all her other distracting thoughts during the afternoon, she almost convinced herself that this was so.

Her hair hung loose and dank upon the shoulder of her dress and had lost the glossy shine which usually set off her pretty head. Her face appeared strained and tired and she had dark shadows under her eyes. She looked across at the old lady on the large bed, the frail lines of the body showed along the soft coverings. Lucile Guyate, the owner of *Wuthering Winds,* was still in a very critical state. Only complete rest and absolutely no excitement of any sort whatsoever, would pull her round.

Margaret started as the door knob turned and the great panels swung slowly inwards. It was only Skeels. She smiled at him and he motioned her not to get up. Picking up a large stool by the chest of drawers and carrying it to the window where she was sitting, he put it down and sat on it, rather like a young boy. For some while there was silence again. The shadows in the room lengthened little by little.

After a while, Skeels said without looking up, "All her life Mrs Guyate has been very good natured. I have been with her for years, Miss, I know. She has been so very trusting that unscrupulous people have often tried to take advantage of her. Whilst the Doctor was alive, of course he used to make sure that such people were not allowed near the place. But since he died, I am afraid there are always many people ready to hang around in case of an opportunity to make something out of Mrs Guyate's kindness. I did my best to keep them away as far as possible but..." he faltered. "There wasn't much I could do."

Skeels' wrinkled old face was a dark shadow. Margaret looked down and saw how he was clasping and unclasping his hands. He was obviously pent up with anguish and was talking to her to rid his thoughts of his memories. She didn't answer him properly because she couldn't think of anything to say, but he seemed content to go on just letting his thoughts take him as they would.

The old butler had not allowed his gaze to deter from his aged mistress on the great bed and he struck Margaret as being slightly pathetic, despite his age and trustworthiness.

Everything was very quiet; nowhere could she hear the slightest sound. The room had now become very shadowy, but Skeels still sat on the stool near old Mrs Guyate who had not stirred. She thought how strange everything was. Had it been possible to surprise her as she was when she first arrived at *Wuthering Winds,* perhaps it would have been the strange silence that would unsettle her the most.

Skeels seemed to have remarkably sharp ears for he heard it first. "The car!" he exclaimed. "They are coming back, Miss."

Margaret reached the front door as the black saloon drew up in the drive with a slight skid on the loose gravel. She was taken aback to see the different car and her breath quickened with fright until she caught sight of Tony. He was grinning at her out of the front window and preparing to jump out. She was so delighted to see him safe and sound that she nearly knocked him over as he emerged from the car. She could not, of course, know of his perils during their short while apart, nor he of hers.

They all proceeded into the house together. The coolness of the evening was settling like a creature by a warm fire. Tony closed the door with a slam and almost simultaneously, came a loud crash from the direction of the library.

Margaret looked dismayed. "Skeels locked Roma Beaumont in the library," she blurted. "She tried to kill me because I found Dr Guyate's body on the stairs in that Chinese vase!"

"What? My darling..." spluttered Tony.

She had not meant to say anything so startling or dramatic, only to make them realise the situation of why Roma Beaumont was locked in the library.

Their words were suddenly punctuated by a series of further loud crashes and the sounds of a heavy object splintering wood. The blows continued for several seconds and then ceased abruptly, leaving dead silence again.

Anthony shot a quick glance at Margaret and moved swiftly along the passage. He found the door of the library still locked, but a reliable, respectful, old voice made him turn.

"Here's the key, Mr Anthony, I have it. I had to lock this vile woman up for reasons I will explain later. Heaven only knows what mischief she's up to now." The wrath was very clear in Skeels' voice in the last sentence.

Anthony took the large iron key and fitted it into the keyhole in the door. The old lock was stiff and its powerful spring took some strength to force it back. With a loud click, it snapped over, and turning the iron ring, Tony swung the door open. The room was quite dark inside. Long shadows threw their hideous bodies across the floor as though bewailing the sinking light.

James Stirling, who was still Wilbur Mortimer to Margaret, stepped past the others into the centre of the room. He glanced quickly about. Nowhere was the tall, slim figure of Roma Beaumont to be seen. The whole group moved into the room when they saw that the medium was not there. Only the rows of dusty books met their surprised gaze.

Without warning, a large form appeared framed in the doorway. With her sleeves rolled to the elbows, a ridiculously large white apron that covered the front of her voluminous person, Mrs Berkley stood with her brawny arms resting upon her hips.

"I'm excusing myself if you please, Sir," she stated in a loud voice, and then glanced around apprehensively as she saw everybody looking at her curiously. She continued in a lower tone, addressing herself to Tony. "I wondered what all the banging was about. Oh! I see —" She broke off with a look of puzzlement on her broad face.

All the others turned to follow the direction of her gaze. The large, glass panelled door leading out into the cool, quiet evening of the garden stood before them as a shattered remnant. Broken glass lay like a sea all around the base of the doors and a long, heavy poker lay abandoned among the shards. Several of the oak latticework pieces had been smashed in half and a hole, large enough to pass a human body through, had been brazenly hacked out of the French windows.

It was clear Roma had no wish to prolong her stay at *Wuthering Winds* any further. Despite the old house's efforts to hold her, she had broken out as though in ingratitude, and had caused malicious damage to her benefactor's home.

James Stirling moved across to the doors and examined the fresh blood that was clearly evident upon the jagged edge of the glass around the hole in the French windows. He straightened up and announced with some gravity, "She's cut herself, legs I think, pretty badly too."

After a moment of silence, Margaret said in amazement, "Mr Mortimer! What? I thought – that is –"

Tony broke in with a grin, "It's alright, you see Mr Wilbur Mortimer is no more. He is really a detective from Scotland Yard who had to work down here in connection with all this business. He assumed the character of an American, an insurance salesman, just to put everyone off their guard. It would have been silly to announce himself and what he was, wouldn't it?"

Margaret was completely taken aback. Even the usually unperturbable Skeels seemed astounded at the news. It took quite a bit more explaining, but while this was going on, the now accepted James Stirling proceeded to examine the broken doors. He opened them completely after retrieving the key from Skeels' possession, and for several minutes he disappeared out into the garden.

It was fairly chilly outside but James did not notice this for he was burning with an idea that had taken root in his mind. He continued to search around for some time before finally returning to the library.

The excitement caused by the sudden change of character had to some extent died down by the time James Stirling had re-entered the room. Mrs Berkley had returned to her domestic duties and also to attend to Mrs Guyate. Skeels was busy collecting the strewn pieces of broken glass. They all looked up when James came in.

"There's a chance," he said, "that Roma has been unable to get far. She seems pretty badly cut, judging by all the blood out there. It's a fact that I could pin quite a bit on her, and she betrays her own guilt by running out. I am going after her. It's a lovely night and there is a trail of blood right across the lawn – she should be easy to follow."

Margaret said nothing. All she wanted was that everything in this terrible experience should end and that she could have Tony to herself again. No more danger or horror lurking round the corner every other minute.

Anthony, however, was keen to join the inspector in following the diminutive clues that they had already picked up. Tony nodded eagerly and was pleased to see James' look of appreciation, as though his support really meant something.

To Tony's mind, it seemed that the whole affair was split into two groups. One concerned the strange footsteps on the stairs, and the rapping on the panels during the night, coupled with all the mystery of the embalmed body of Doctor Herbert Guyate. The other dealt with the personage of Roma Beaumont, and her part in the whole affair. *If only something could be found to link the two together*, he thought, *they would at least be able to start at a definite point and follow up each observation until the whole picture was complete.*

"Before we start," went on James, looking at Margaret, "there's just one thing I think we'll clear up right now. You say, my dear, that the body of Herbert Guyate was in the Chinese vase on the stairs?"

She nodded her head and stirred uneasily in the chair she was seated in, as though the memory brought back a terribly vivid thought, as well it did.

"Then what you saw must still be in the vase?"

"Yes, I didn't dare to look again, but I think Skeels saw it after he had put Roma Beaumont in here."

James looked at Skeels questioningly. The butler had glanced up upon hearing his name mentioned. "Yes, that's right, Sir," he said quietly, "it certainly is a horrible sight."

Anthony had risen knowing what was expected of him and now he followed the detective out of the room along the passage to the stairs in silence.

The hall they noticed had a faint, unaccountable scent, and as they mounted the stairs it grew steadily stronger and more pungent. The odour seemed to have pervaded the whole area. At the landing they stopped and Tony saw how James did not stop to think, but walked straight up to the great piece of pottery and peered inside – a practice born of habit! Tony followed his example.

The sight that met his eyes made his nerves reel. Stuffed down into the vase, the body was twisted and bent. The leering face was turned upwards and the sightless eyes stared heavenward. The little grey beard jutted forward obtrusively.

James's voice recalled him to his senses. "Notice the beard, my friend." Anthony looked puzzled. "No piece is ripped away," remarked the Yard man significantly.

They returned to the hall where James picked up one of the rugs on the floor, and running upstairs, threw it over the top of the vase. Then he rejoined Anthony. "At least that's one part of the business over," he said, "one more clue should end everything."

When that last thing did come, it was so completely unexpected, that everyone was knocked off their balance. The last great surprise that *Wuthering Winds* had in store for them was not far off and it was by far the greatest of all the many strange twists in this whole dreadful affair.

"Well, let's start," urged James. "We'll need as many flashlights as possible. I've got one, has anybody got another?"

The infallible Skeels appeared from the library, "There's an old bicycle lamp in the kitchen, Sir," he announced and promptly disappeared to get it.

Margaret, looking extremely tired and strained, told them she intended to accompany them. "But that's ridiculous, darling," said Tony gently. "You're tired out and I think you've had enough for one day." But she was insistent, so they had to finally agree. Tony went up to get her coat and at last they were ready.

They left the house from the French windows of the library. The garden was as quiet and still as the grave and the fragrance of foliage hung around them. Just the softest sound could be heard of gnats in clustering hoards suspended in the air. The evening gloom encased the grounds with a twinge of added mystery.

The little party shone their torches on the ground, picking out the large spots of fresh, wet blood that lay mingling with the damp dew on the springy turf. A light, warm breeze rippled the trees by the tennis courts as it swung down from the Downs. The trail of blood led directly to the wire door in the netting around the courts, and almost as soon as they passed through, Margaret knew where they would end. She thought of her first experience down here on the courts when the strange woman had first appeared to her from out of the bushes. She had wondered at the time what she was doing. Now she could hazard a pretty shrewd guess.

A soft moon sailed lazily across the clear June skies. The hills in the distance loomed huge and grey. Skeels let out a low wheeze as he shone his enormous, old-fashioned torch on the ground and along the edge of the tennis court. The soft rustle of the great laurel bushes outside the wire fencing caused them all to glance up swiftly.

Not one of them had any inkling of what to expect, but a certainty of the end to the whole dreadful mystery was in all of their minds. The spots of liquid that guided their path lead round the fence and along the back of the court immediately to the small pavilion. A fresh crimson spot on the single, low step indicated the place where Roma Beaufort had fled. Margaret could not help but think of the willpower that must have been exercised to carry the woman in her poor condition so far from the house.

Outside the little wooden building, the party of people gathered in a group, momentarily uncertain as to what to do. Here again, James Stirling displayed his prowess of decision making.

"Either side of the door," he murmured, signalling them into position. Taking Skeels' heavy torch, he shone it full upon the narrow door. The glass of the window reflected the beams. The man who had so cleverly portrayed himself as an American stepped forward, and with a significantly quick motion, turned the handle and flung open the door with a loud crash. He directed the light of the torch into the room only to be met by the dank gloom of the confined and empty space. With a swift bound, he sprang inside the little shack.

Margaret stood petrified outside and listened to the tramp of the boots on the wooden floor boards. After a few seconds, James reappeared in the doorway. "No sign in here," he announced and his voice trembled slightly, they all knew he was disappointed.

"Just a minute, Sir," growled Skeels. "Perhaps I can show you a possible hiding place." Nobody spoke as the tall, drooping figure stepped up to the door. James followed the butler back into the pavilion. Tony caught Margaret around the waist as they followed them in.

A number of trunks and boxes were arranged against the wooden walls of the little hut. At one corner several boxes were stacked on an old chest bearing the letters *Croquet*. James handed the lamp to the butler. They remained perfectly silent for a full minute at least. Skeels' huge flashlight thrashed to and fro stabbing at the dark corner. Anthony was watching Skeels' wrinkled face. He suddenly seemed to become very old. He was like a man performing a duty that he knew would be his last on this earth.

A faint smell of damp, rotting timber carried on the breeze, moving the sleep-drugged foliage outside in restless motion. Finally, the fishing beam of the torch came to rest on the old chest. Slowly the circle of light was raised higher and higher, illuminating in turn the pile of boxes – four in total, but still the beam rose. Up the peeling wall to the edge of the low roof then across the slanting roofing boards until it suddenly shone full upon a square trapdoor in the roof. The dust on the little door was smeared as though it had recently been removed and readjusted.

Tony saw Skeels' watery eyes glow brightly with some deep mixed emotion that was unfathomable. He returned the torch to the detective.

James climbed gingerly upon the stepped boxes and pushed upwards upon the wooden covering of the loft while shining the torch straight up into the blackness. It was then it happened! It was so sudden that the watchers fell back in fright.

James probed the darkness in the loft with the light beam, and for an instant he remained poised, but then uttered a cry of mingled surprise and fear. His heavy body came crashing down! He was on his feet in a split second and retrieving his dropped torch, just managed to catch the outlines of a figure as it hurtled to the ground. The flashlight illuminated a face as it landed, like a panther, waiting to spring.

There was no mistaking the yellowing, parchment-like skin, the stained teeth bared in a snarl and the short, grey beard protruding from the set jaw. It was Herbert Guyate – Terror of *Wuthering Winds* – The Doctor Embalmed.

17

Unmasking the Shadows

The great range of blue-green Downs had the appearance of being wrapped in sleep. The only sign of life on the patchwork earth was the slow moving figure of an old shepherd steadily plodding his way up the naked hillside. At his heels, a shaggy dog made a devoted companion. Nowhere was there a sign of the fold that could be the old man's only care.

The tall, gabled roof of *Wuthering Winds* stood sharply sullen and resentful at the chilled fingers of the summer morning. A large white gull had perched itself precariously on the high red chimney stack, and an innocent baby rabbit nibbled a hurried meal from the crisp, green grass at the fringe of the tennis court behind the line of stately poplars. But it's nervousness was unfounded. There would be no tall woman walking stealthily round the pavilion from behind the thick laurels, on her habitual stroll early in the day.

A hush was holding the world spellbound, trembling on the brink of another day. It was as though the elements were undecided as to how the day should be. A light breeze might carry the clouds scuttling across the sky, leaving the warm sun in possession of the era. On the other hand, a summer storm might break the heatwave that was giving Southern England the warmest summer in years.

A thin shaft of sunlight cut between a gap in the clouds and illuminated the old house. All but one of the rooms on the east and southeast side enjoyed the early warmth. This one room alone was still dark and sombre. However, nearly all the people staying at *Wuthering Winds* were grouped together in this dreary section of the house.

The long, oak panelled library with the crowded rows of glass fronted bookshelves was filled with all the strange people who had pervaded the lovely old country manor house for the last few days. Something had come to pass here, events had been enacted and terrifying experiences lived. The old place had become a tenant of tragedy and a bearer of misery. People's lives had been influenced and changed. Some things would never be the same again.

Anthony was sitting in a deep armchair. His brow was puckered and he was evidently thinking hard. On the arm of the chair, Margaret had perched her slim figure and although she looked tired and worried, there was also a look of relief, as though some great worry had been removed from her mind.

Standing quietly in front of the broken panes of the great French windows, was the neat butler. Always discreet, dear old Skeels was gazing before him with a fixed perplexity. Next to him stood Mrs Berkley, who cut a quaint character in a wide check skirt and blouse, surmounted by an enormous patchwork shawl. She had, through force of habit, crossed her arms in the kind of attitude she might take up whilst placing an order with the grocer's boy at the back door. But the person or rather the persons who held her awed regard were not of any such character.

Dark and sullen, but still with the dangerous glint of menace in her downcast eyes, sat Roma Beaumont with her legs propped up on the couch. She studied the strips of white linen which bound her calves and knee. Deep, red stains showed through the bandages administered roughly but thoroughly by Wilbur Mortimer, alias James Stirling.

With his broad back straight and a look of antagonised concentration, the strange character around whom the whole mystery of *Wuthering Winds* revolved, sat in a great high back chair slightly to the right of Roma Beaumont.

The unusual parchment like texture of his pallid, yellowing skin gave him the terrible look of one returned from the grave. The sharply pointed iron grey beard and trimmed moustache were intact and well kept but for one part. Here, the side of the jaw where the shorter hair tapered the beard, a bloody mess showed where a wrench of the fibres had torn the growth from the unfortunate man's chin.

For a brief period, none of the people in the library spoke. Each looked at the other with mingled uncertainty and doubt. Eventually, James Stirling rose to his feet and addressed the whole room.

"All of you – my friends – I think that this whole dreadful and terrifying business is at an end, but before we can turn a new page in the book of our lives, some extraordinary, important and vital explanations and consequent decisions must be made. This is *my* idea, so as I am the first to put forward the suggestion, I will take it on myself to be the first to speak and tell you my identity and purpose in this house."

The little man paused to reflect on the best method to commence his narrative. "I am Detective Inspector James Stirling of New Scotland Yard C.I.D. I was idling my time in London when information of a personal nature reached me concerning a certain individual who was attempting to enter Great Britain under an assumed name. This man was known to the police in connection with a particular case of impersonation and unproven robbery on a grand scale, a matter of some fourteen years ago.

I was of course at the time a young man still on patrol beat, but I could dimly remember the extraordinary case of the Duchess of Whymple's formal dinner party in commemoration of her daughter's twenty-first birthday. The great affair was held in London on the 23rd of September 1929."

James thrust a hand into his pocket and from his wallet extracted a slip of tinted paper. It was a closely printed newspaper clipping which he consulted from time to time as he proceeded with his story.

"The Duchess, who lived at Thorptone in Derbyshire when she was not in London, had become friendly with a certain doctor – Dr Herbert Guyate, who ran a very profitable and extremely neighbourly practice in the small, well-to-do town nearby. And so, it was natural that the doctor should receive an invitation to the celebration in London. The doctor, finding himself indisposed, sent a request to his twin brother in Westminster to call on the Duchess and present her daughter with some form of gift, and to make apologies for his brother's non-attendance.

Now Mr. Wilfred Julian Guyate was a man of mean position and doubtful resources. His main vice being gambling and drinking. Of late, he had been under the influence of some particularly disreputable characters to whom he owed money and they saw this as an opportunity to make use of the honourable Mr Wilfred Guyate in exchange for a release from his debts.

So, it was Mr Wilfred Guyate posing as his brother, of whom he was a remarkable likeness, who went to the Duchess's party in the identity of the doctor. During the celebration however, he abducted himself, along with a splendid collection of precious jewellery including part of the Duchess' daughter's gifts. During dinner he had taken fright at being introduced to the private detective employed to guard the valuables and subsequently bolted.

The police never had any doubts as to who the thief was, but were unable to contact the man in question until a certain individual left the country under an assumed name. When facts were at last proved, he had made good his escape and the police were compelled to abandon the case for the time being.

Mr Herbert Guyate, with his devoted wife, were afterwards compelled to leave the county of Derbyshire owing to the unpleasantness and snobbery of the members of Thorptone, brought on by the scandal of the events and their relationship to the suspected man. They eventually settled here in Sussex where their past was unknown and where the good doctor spent the few last remaining years of his life."

The speaker paused to reflect, taking a deep breath as he gathered his thoughts. The silence in the room felt thick and suffocating.

"Where I fit into the picture is at a period some six months ago. We received information that this particular man was in London and in contact with a woman of no small repute, in circles connected with spiritualists and mediumistic science. We were curious, but typical of the British tradition, did not interfere but bided our time, hardly believing that the man was anything but what he appeared.

Meanwhile, the whole case was being carefully reviewed and pieced together. It was as though we were spinning a web around our man, unknown to himself, he was under almost constant observation. Finally, we were ready. Then came the unexpected: the woman had managed to worm her way into the confidence of Mrs Lucile Guyate and had gone down to Sussex to take up her abode in the old lady's house!

At the same time, the man known to us as Wilfred Julian Guyate, disappeared. Events had moved too quickly and we had lost contact with our man. Our only hope was to follow up the woman. The events in connection with the parties concerned were too much of a coincidence to be disregarded. The plan was formed. In the guise of an American insurance agent, I was to somehow gain access to the house. Working on my own, I was hoping to pick up a clue as to the whereabouts of Wilfred Guyate. Just what a hornets' nest I ran into, as you all know! So, I think if you could be persuaded to comply," said James, turning to the bearded man sitting motionless with bowed head, "it would be to our mutual advantage."

The man now revealed as the deceased Doctor Herbert Guyate's twin brother did not answer for a full minute. Then he turned to the slim, dark woman on the couch by his side and in a tired voice said, "I'm going to tell them everything, Roma? Don't you think it would be better? It will all have to come out now anyway."

The woman did not answer but her complexion had turned a shade paler and her hand trembled slightly as she made an incoherent gesture.

Wilfred Guyate rose to his feet. He squared his broad shoulders and although he looked tired and haggard, he seemed to have taken on a new air, as if a confession would relieve a weight from his mind that had been an intolerable burden.

"There is just one thing I will request, Inspector," he said thickly, "and that is that I may give my explanation in the presence of my sister-in-law?"

James Stirling looked inquiringly at the two servants. The old butler understood the question before it was asked. He turned and spoke a few inaudible words to Mrs Berkley who nodded her head as if in consent. Skeels spoke in a high, thin voice, the strain of the night's events was clearly beginning to tell on the plucky, old butler. "Alright," he said simply, "but not too long please."

Margaret sat transfixed by the revelations of the last few minutes. She noted with curiosity how strangely this whole affair was developing, but the horrible suspicion of Wilfred Guyate's evil intent was like a germinating seed in her mind. She couldn't gather an atom of pity for the dead doctor's twin brother.

With the exception of Roma Beaumont, they all stood up. They moved towards the door, with Wilfred Guyate leading the way, and James Stirling following behind. Just before they passed through, the detective half turned and requested that Mrs Berkley should stay behind with the spiritualist. The glint in the good woman's eye left him in no doubt as to the effectiveness of the vigil.

Out of the library and along the passage they proceeded, into the hall and to the base of the great oak stairs. Margaret looked at the huge carved stair post and marvelled at the things that had come to pass since she had first noticed the queer markings on the wood. As they climbed the stairs, one behind the other, they trod quietly as though they were afraid of waking someone sleeping nearby. Each one of them seemed to notice the irony of this as they reached the little landing and passed by the voluminous Chinese vase that stood with the rug still covering its ghastly contents.

The hair on the girl's neck prickled slightly as the dreadful memories once more invaded her mind. Tony seemed to sense her fear for he caught her cold hand and together they continued to the landing above.

A thin light streamed in from the narrow openings in the thick panelled walls. The bolt studded doors were all closed as though each one hid the secrets of its past within.

Before one such door they paused in a little group. Skeels stepped forward, and tapping lightly on the heavy panelling, turned the ring and swung the door slowly inwards.

18

Last of the Line

Brother and sister-in-law faced each other across the wide, dim room. Mrs Lucile Guyate propped up in bed by pillows, looked frail and extremely fatigued. Her eyes however, had taken on a look of keen intellectual intensity. Her face had the appearance of transparent beeswax and the wisps of grey hair that fell across her broad forehead were withered and dry.

Wilfred did not move. He stood leaning towards her, staring at her, with one hand raised slightly as if he was about to outstretch it towards the old lady. Level-eyed, they regarded each other. Lucile Guyate was the first to speak. Her voice was even and she spoke calmly, without emotion. It was as though she knew she had to conserve her strength.

"Wilfred! So, it *is* you." The man inclined his head in acknowledgement but he did not answer.

"Whilst I have been lying here, I have thought things over. I think I know just why you came back. Wilfred, you came to *Wuthering Winds* to kill me, didn't you?"

The man did not move.

"You have been abroad for so long, Wilfred. You thought I might have forgotten you? Well in a way, you were right. I did forget, but when I saw you last night, I suddenly realised just what was going on."

The invalid paused, her voice trembled slightly on the last few words. She closed her sunken eyes and drew a deep breath, composing herself before she continued.

"You must have suddenly remembered while you were away that my husband had accumulated quite considerable wealth while he was alive. When you heard news of his death, which no doubt reached you after a time, you hit upon the plan which you have been carrying out here." The old lady's voice was suddenly icy. "You had a clever brain Wilfred; I always said you could have been a success if only you had put your mind to something. I suppose you met this woman, Roma Beaumont, and she entered into your plan. You got her to worm her way into my confidence, interest me in her spiritual ideas and finally get herself an invitation to my home here. Then you were to appear, pose as my husband and inflict fear into me. Eventually, the strain would kill me by hastening the reactions of my heart, which you remembered had always been weak."

A certain harshness was creeping into the old lady's tone, she was talking quickly now as though she knew she had little time. "You took a photograph of my dear husband from my room here, so that you could compare your likeness to him. Am I right?"

He remained silent and still, making no movement except for his eyes, which had dropped to the floor at the foot of the bed.

"You removed the body of my husband from down-stairs, and then you walked up to my room and tapped on the panels. When you came in, I struck a match to light a candle, and it was then that I saw you. Of course, your devilish scheme worked, and I had the worst heart attack I have ever had. Unfortunately, I re-covered. No doubt you would have tried again, but my other guests..." The old lady made a gesture appearing to notice the other people in the room for the first time, "...have in some way interfered. For that I am deeply grateful to them."

It was plain that Mrs Guyate was finding the exer-tion too much for her. Her head lolled back against the snowy pillows and her eyes were closed. Her breath was coming in a short, sharp motion. Skeels moved round to the side of the bed, but the old lady heard him and without opening her eyes, she raised a hand just a few inches from the bedspread to restrain him. After a while she looked again at the still figure of her brother-in-law.

"Wilfred, am I right?"

Silence filled the room.

"Have you nothing to say to me?"

The man spoke for the first time in a dull, listless voice. It was evident he was struck by the startling accuracy of Lucile's accusations. His tone was husky as he said, "Lucile, there is nothing I can say except that Roma is my wife –"

Margaret gasped involuntarily.

"Wilfred," the old lady now had difficulty in speaking, her breathing was just a series of short gasps. "Go down to the library – in the desk – something – go now. Quickly..."

The man made no movement.

Her voice was low and faint but strangely firm, almost commanding. "Wilfred, *GO!*"

Very slowly, as though undecided what he should do, the bearded man backed to the door. On the threshold he regarded his sister-in-law intently, his face working in a peculiar fashion, tiny beads of glistening sweat showing on his forehead. Without a word he turned and left the room.

Tony started forward fearing lest the man should escape, but James signalled to let him go. Lucile Guyate started speaking again. "My nephew?" Tony went up and took her cold hand. "Yesterday I had my will destroyed. I had left everything to Roma Beaumont's spiritual society, which of course was what my wicked brother-in-law wanted."

Her old face was filled with emotion, her hand feebly attempting to clasp Tony's a little tighter as though she feared he might go before she had finished.

"I made another will – Skeels and the doctor witnessed it – I left everything to you and Margaret, I hope you will be very happy, dears."

Margaret was sobbing silently; Tony's eyes were misty.

The cold hand dropped to the white sheets, the grey head lolled sideways, Mrs Lucile Guyate filled her lungs for the last time.

From downstairs came the sharp report of a single revolver shot.

19

Plans Beyond the Horizon

The sound of clattering hooves and the rattle of iron-shod wheels gradually receded into the distance. The village carter's neat trap, drawn by a thin but well-groomed pony, looked well loaded. In the back sat Roma Beaumont, and opposite her was James Stirling, sitting on the large trunk among other smaller suitcases. Both were sitting very straight. The woman did not look back once. Her lips were tightly compressed but although she held her head high, there was an air of sulkiness, as though the very trees and green fields they passed held her in disgrace.

Tony and Margaret stood in the driveway watching her go. As the sound of the horse and trap faded into the distance, they turned and re-entered the old house. The recent grimness of its strange occupants had cast a noticeable melancholy over the place in the last few days.

They went out onto the veranda, and in the warm air, Tony held the girl in his arms and kissed her lightly on the lips.

"It's all over darling. James will see Roma Beaumont on the train and we will never hear of her again."

"I hope not," shuddered Margaret.

"You need not worry, my sweet, James was right, the woman has had too much of a shock to ever cause any such trouble again. If he had exposed her, the proceedings would have been so involved that the case would have dragged on for months. This place would have been besieged with newspaper people and inquisitive, morbid-minded sightseers. Besides, you and I would have been obliged to frequent the courts and the publicity and scandal would have made this little bit of old-world Sussex practically untenable by any decent folk."

Margaret nodded mutely, her blue-grey eyes glistening with moisture as she trembled, "And what about – about Mrs Guyate's – er – will?"

He held her at arm's length and scanned the puzzled sweetness of her face, "It's alright," he answered gently, "she has left *Wuthering Winds* to us."

"Tony," the girl replied quietly, "I could never bear to live here – after –" she broke off and buried her head in his shoulder.

"You won't have to, darling! I'll get rid of it and we'll go back to London and have a charming flat of our own, somewhere just off Kensington Gardens, perhaps?"

She looked up at him and smiled. He pulled her close and looked over her mop of curls at the great hills beyond. After a pause, she wondered, "Why did Wilfred Guyate shoot himself?"

"My dear old aunt knew that gun was in that desk. She relied on the man's last vestige of family honour to surface, hoping it would drive him to erase the stain of dishonour on the Guyate name." He paused and studied the lush garden. "From Wilfred's point of view, I think he knew that the old lady would die and I suppose he thought that it was the easiest way out. Besides that, he was probably rather influenced with emotion. Anyway, it has saved everyone from a most horribly unpleasant time and I believe he is better off."

He ended suddenly and raised her face to his, "Look!" he exclaimed, "the sun is breaking through – it's going to be a lovely day."

20

The End of the Trail

Kensington Gardens and Hyde Park, in the heart of noisy London, was like a corner of Kent on this basking July afternoon. The Serpentine was dotted with boats and skiffs. People sat everywhere – middle aged and elderly on the numerous seats, and the young and romantic sprawled out on the grass in the shade of the giant trees. Everywhere the greenness relieved the heat of the day.

Down the wide, shadowed path, a young couple walked arm in arm. The girl in a light, summer frock kept glancing up with admiration at the tall, fair-haired figure of her husband. They paid no heed to the casual glances of the people resting on either side of the avenue, oblivious to everything and everyone but each other.

Suddenly, however, they stopped dead and stared in surprise! A plump man sat on a park bench deep in thought. He seemed to be meditating and pondering on a subject alien to other people's thoughts. He had not noticed the two young people and gave no sign of recognition until they stood before him.

"James!"

The little man started violently and then, with an exclamation of pleasure, he stood up and grasped a hand in each of his own.

"My dears!" his face beamed with genuine pleasure at seeing them both.

For a while they chatted together exchanging news and greetings. Then reminiscences crept into their conversation and a certain note of sadness came into his voice as Anthony related how he had sold *Wuthering Winds* and come back to live in a flat just across the road from Kensington Gardens.

"You must come back for tea, James," invited Margaret warmly. As they walked along, the detective revealed that he was really trying to solve a problem in a case he was working on at present.

"But I've never yet, certainly never again, come up against a case like the mystery of Herbert Guyate's body," he added frankly.

"Anyway, it's finished forever now," waved Margaret, trying to dismiss the subject.

"There was only one point that was never cleared up," interrupted Tony. "Do you remember the note that the poor housemaid slipped into my hand as I went into dinner that fateful night, just before we found her out on the veranda?"

James, after thinking, said that he recalled the note quite clearly.

"Well, why did she want me to meet her in the garden that night? Did she really know something or –"

James' laugh cut him short, "I admit that it puzzled me for a bit, but eventually I realised that the whole thing was just an odd coincidence." He grinned at Margaret, "I think she was completely infatuated with you, Anthony. She probably just thought that her turn for romance had come." He added seriously, "She must have met Wilfred Guyate in the garden and died of shock when she thought it was Dr Guyate back from the grave! Anyway!" he relapsed. "You'd better watch him, my dear!"

"I will," chuckled Margaret with a mischievous wink.

As they crossed the road, a black London taxi narrowly missed them. The great city's roar seemed to diminish the significance of everyone within it.

Afterword

By the time I was old enough to remember my holidays with my grandparents, they had retired to Derbyshire, England. I would be flown in from South Africa, where I grew up, to spend happy summers picking blackberries, finding hedgehogs and visiting museums. They had led extraordinary lives and relics from their adventures decorated their charming country cottage in the Peak District. I have clear memories of the stories my grandfather would tell me about the Tibetan prayer wheel, the elaborately sheaved kukri, the boxed and pinned butterflies and the exotic paintings that hung on their walls. My imagination would soar with the enchanting stories of foreign lands and adventures, but at the centre of it all would be my very British and rather fearless grandparents.

My grandfather, Captain David Wilson Fletcher, volunteered for the Commandos which later became the

SAS regiments and paratrooper brigades. He saw action in France and Germany in the last year of the WW2, and after VE day, was seconded to War Tribunal duties in Germany.

He was then commissioned and served with 2nd Battalion 7th Gurkha Rifles attaining the rank of Captain in 1946. With his Gurkha troops, he carried out the harrowing duties of escorting the last partition refugee trains from West Bengal (Pakistan) to Delhi in newly independent India in 1947.

While on leave, my grandfather attended a dance near Leigh-on-Sea at a nurses' residence. A particularly beautiful nurse caught his eye and my grandparents' lives were intertwined from that day onwards.

With the war behind them, they bade farewell to Great Britain and embarked on a life of travel and adventure. They went to Cairo, Egypt, in response to a Times advert for an English and PE teacher at Alexander College. My grandmother became matron at Heliopolis Hospital and then a while later, they welcomed their first daughter, Melody. My grandfather enjoyed writing and became a regular short story contributor to Blackwood's magazine and The Illustrated London News.

But his love for India and Nepal was in my grandfather's bones and when in 1950 he saw a recruitment advert from Finlays for a tea planter role in Darjeeling, with required knowledge of the Nepali language, he could not resist. They had twelve years of remarkable life in this remote corner below the Himalayas and welcomed two more daughters into their family. My grandfather's writing continued and he documented their lives in his first book called '*The Children of Kanchenjunga*', published by Constable in 1955.

With Chinese threats looming through neighbouring Tibet in 1962, he decided to try his luck in Africa. The next eight years were spent planting tea in Nyasaland. As an ex British Army officer, my grandfather was drafted to assist in independence ceremonies in Nyasaland when the Queen Mother visited to create the new Malawi.

My grandparents then set their sights on Malta as a place to retire and for my grandfather to pursue his love of writing. They built a beautiful villa with an ocean view for inspiration. Clearly not ready for retirement, they embarked on a new project and opened a public aquarium, which soon became one of the first dolphinariums. It became a family affair and when their daughters were home from nursing training in Salisbury, they helped with dolphin training and performances. The political scene of Malta changed, seeing the British swiftly removed. With characteristic British commando training and courage, my grandfather smuggled the dolphins out and before long had re-established the dolphin show on the beach in Durban, South Africa.

By this time, my mother (Melody) and father had met and fallen in love. Their wedding was a happy occasion and included a dolphin bridesmaid! Soon thereafter I was born and adapted to life by the dolphin pools. My grandfather grew the show to include a full size replica of the Dromedaris sailing ship which brought the first Dutch settlers to South Africa. But this was only partly successful, and when the dolphins died from human influenza, it was time to quit Africa too.

My grandmother had special childhood memories of her time in Derbyshire as an evacuee, so they decided to retire again, and use this beautiful part of England as inspiration for writing once more. Wherever they lived in these later years, they always had the most exquisite gardens. Having lived a life of growing plants and projects, it was no surprise that they created enchanting spaces of natural beauty. Their last cottage was on a popular walking route in the Peak District and was often photographed and painted. It was called Rose Cottage and was covered in a pink rambling rose.

My grandmother passed away peacefully in 2015 and my grandfather joined her in 2019, both well past their ninetieth year.

How does one pack up lives lived so brightly?

As we held my grandparents' precious items and remembered the stories and shared moments, we realised that the brightness never fades. We carry the light within ourselves – inside our memories.

Among their things we found boxes of my grandfather's writing. Bundles of first and second drafts with pencil notes up and down the margins; thin sheaves of paper, all typed out by typewriter! It has taken us some time to go through it all, and to our delight, we have found some unpublished pieces. Doctor Embalmed was one of them. So, here's some of the brightness for you to share in.

We suspect this was written during the India years, in the 1950s, judging by the references to clothes, authors and other small details. It's been tidied up a bit and edited, but the story and writing remains true to the original style. Doctor Embalmed falls into the vintage horror genre and is quite different to the other stories that my grandfather had published during his writing career. But I hope Doctor Embalmed brings delight to fans of this genre today.

Natalie Knox

About the author

 D.W. Fletcher volunteered for the commandos during WW2 and was then commissioned and served with 2nd Battalion 7th Gurkha Rifles attaining the rank of Captain in 1946. His life thereafter took him on great adventures to Egypt, India, Malawi, Malta and South Africa. He returned to Great Britain and retired to the Peak District in Derbyshire. The backdrop to his life was his passion for writing and he took inspiration from the people he met and cultures he lived in. In 1955, while in India, he authored *Children of Kanchenjunga*. He was a regular contributor to Blackwood's magazine, Times of India, Illustrated London News and Derbyshire Life magazine.